LEAVING CLOVERTON

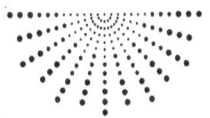

EMI HILTON

5 PRINCE PUBLISHING
5PRINCEBOOKS.COM

Published by 5 PRINCE PUBLISHING & BOOKS, LLC

PO Box 865, Arvada, CO 80001

www.5PrinceBooks.com

ISBN digital: 978-1-63112-364-1

ISBN print: 978-1-63112-365-8

Cover Credit: Marianne Nowicki

04232024.1

For Mom and Dad

ACKNOWLEDGMENTS

I am forever in debt to my readers. Thank you for following me on my writing journey, for purchasing my books, leaving five-star reviews, and sharing with a friend. I couldn't be an author without you. Your support means everything to me.

To my publisher, 5 Prince Books. Thank you for believing in me and my writing. I am beyond grateful that my story found a home at your publishing house. I appreciate your guidance and encouragement. You will never know the depth of my gratitude. It truly is an honor to work with you.

To my editor, Cate Byers who inspires me. A huge heartfelt appreciation to you for your enlightenment in helping my words and story come to life. You are truly a gifted and talented person. Thank you for your patience as you helped me to improve my story.

To my copy editor, Jessica Mehring. Thank you for catching my many mistakes, pointing out my weakness with grace, and helping me improve and grow as a writer. Thanks a million.

To my husband, Tyler. My forever companion and friend. My one true love. I love you more every day. Thank you for believing in me. With you by my side, I know every dream is within reach.

To my parents, siblings, extended family, and friends. My life is more beautiful with all of you in it. I appreciate your continued love and support. My heart is full as I think of each of you. I am blessed to have all of you in my life. I hope you all know how much you mean to me.

Last, I thank God, my faithful Father in Heaven. All good things truly come from thee. I thank thee for giving me the words to write when I needed them. I am grateful for the desire you have planted in my heart to improve and grow in my craft. I praise thy name and devote all the glory and honor to thee. I hope all will come to know of your redeeming goodness and grace.

LEAVING CLOVERTON

CHAPTER ONE

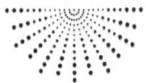

"The GPS says we're almost there. Is this home for you?" the Uber driver asked, making eye contact with Rachel through the rearview mirror. "I don't get many requests from the airport to Cloverton."

Rachel could only imagine. Her speck of a town, in the middle of flyover country, had little to offer, along with an even smaller population. Most used the two lane highway as a convenient thoroughfare as they drove onto more exciting cities like St. Louis or Des Moines. Cloverton, yeah, it wasn't any sort of destination at all, not for anyone but those returning home to visit family.

Soon, peeking out on the horizon, the outline of homes and farms came into view. All recognizable because nothing had changed. It was like someone had snapped a photo fifty years ago and placed it at the back of a scrapbook. Cloverton had carbon-copy brick buildings which hugged each other, lining both sides of Main Street. A one-room, white-painted library gave a touch of variety to the landscape. Rachel remembered the two over-sized chairs facing the front window, where she had devoured stacks of books before filling up her wagon with new ones to take home.

The mom-and-pop grocery store, which only had handheld baskets and no pushcarts, was where she worked as a bagger at sixteen. Next to the K-12 school was the coveted sports stadium, where the high school played their home games, and where she had her first kiss under the bleachers. All the memories came back with a vengeance, some good and some bad. It had been so long since she had returned, and it would probably be years before she ever came back again.

But was this home?

The streets were familiar, but the buildings looked dingier than she remembered. Was Main Street only two blocks? That couldn't possibly be right, but apparently, it was. Then Rachel recalled all over again why she had left in the first place.

Pushing up her chin, Rachel shook her head. "Not anymore." She peered out the passenger side window, wringing her jittery hands together. The boring structures passed right on by. "It hasn't been for years."

The Uber driver gave a curt nod, ending their very brief exchange of words.

Then, at the top of the hill, the hotel came into view. It had a banquet room, the only big gathering place in town, where every major dance, graduation, and event of her life had been held. Here was also the location of this weekend's ten-year high school reunion.

Her heart thundered to a steady staccato beat. Fumbling around, she dug into her purse, retrieving her trusty compact. Flipping it open, she scanned her makeup, scrutinizing every inch of her face. Rachel had one shot to change the narrative in her less-than-adequate love life. This weekend was going to be the beginning of her love story. Wishful thinking? Probably. But then again, she had always been a bit of an optimist.

Back in high school, Rachel had blown it. Chickened out,

essentially, but . . . that was Ten-Years-Ago Rachel. Today's Rachel would be charming and self-assured. If ever there was time to flip the script, that was this weekend. For ten years she had lived with regrets, not anymore. The RSVP list had one name on it she cared about: Brandon Belford. Just thinking about him now made her palms sweaty and cheeks flushed. Through the grapevine, she learned he was newly divorced and . . . available.

Coming to a halt in front of the hotel, the Uber driver peered over his shoulder at her in the back seat. "This is you." He opened his door, climbing out.

"Great." Rachel applied one last dab of lip gloss, smacking her lips together. She tossed it back into her purse. "Thanks."

Exiting the vehicle, the summer air, all muggy and sticky like cotton candy, engulfed her entire being. An instant trickle of sweat dripped down her back. Yeah, this was Cloverton.

"Oh, great," Rachel mumbled as she grabbed her roller suit-case from the Uber driver, who had set it on the curb. "My hair is going to be flat."

He hesitated, eyeing her.

She waved off her comment meant only for herself. He left without another word. Her summer dress stuck to her skin, making her feel awkward. Rachel tried her best to air it out by pulling the front of her dress away from her skin. Then she moved it back and forth to create more air flow.

Muttering under her breath, "Ahh—it's useless." She threw her hands up.

Up before the crack of dawn, Rachel had spent the better part of the morning carefully curling her hair into soft beachy waves. Then at the airport, she had double checked to ensure it had maintained its style. Now she had flat, sweaty hair. *This is great. Just great. Brandon will take one look at me and move right along to someone else.*

Brandon wasn't just any guy, he was *the* guy. Always the lead.

Never the supporting actor. And one didn't win over a guy like him if they were playing in the minor leagues.

Her phone rang, interrupting her spiraling thoughts. Rachel fished her cell phone out of her purse and tapped to accept the call. Placing it up to her ear, she said, "Haley. Are you already here?" She scanned the front of the lobby.

Her purse slipped down from her shoulder, and Rachel hiked it back up. All around her, people were entering and exiting the hotel. The hotel probably had more visitors today than it had all the other days of the year combined. She smiled at a few recognizable faces who brushed past her.

"No," Haley sighed. "My flight was delayed. I snagged another flight, and I'm about to board. I'll be there soon. The flight is only two hours."

Rachel glanced at her watch. "Bummer. I guess I'll get checked in, but I'll wait until you get here to eat dinner. Does that sound okay?"

"Yes, I'll be hungry and ready to eat by the time I arrive." Haley paused, then lowered her voice. "Have you seen Brandon yet?"

"No. Not yet." Rachel scrutinized the people entering and exiting the hotel, hoping for a glimpse of Brandon. Fiddling with her hair, she then covered her mouth with her hand to muffle her voice. "But . . . he did RSVP. He's coming."

Depending on a ten-year high school reunion to rewrite the past wasn't exactly . . . original. If anything, Rachel knew she was teetering ever so close to pathetic. But it wasn't like this plan had come completely out of left field. Back during her senior year, Rachel had shared a moment with Brandon. It was a missed opportunity, causing her years of regret. Enough already.

"He wouldn't miss it. I know Brandon." Haley's tone turned slightly mocking. "He's probably been counting down the days until the reunion, so he can once again bask in the glory and adoration of every single woman in our graduating class."

"Hey," Rachel scoffed, examining the front of her dress again. She picked off some stray lint with her free hand. "I'm one of those women."

"I know. I know. I just don't want you to be disappointed if the weekend doesn't go the way you planned." Haley cleared her throat, then paused. Finally she added, "Besides, this is the first time I'm leaving my baby. I'm thrilled I get to be around some other adults for a change, especially you. Try not to spend the entire weekend upset if Brandon is flirting with everyone else, too."

Rachel knew the transition to motherhood had been extra challenging for Haley when she had Elsa. She had expressed feeling isolated and lost in her new role. Being a single person, Rachel had no idea how to relate to Haley's struggles, but she could guarantee Haley had an enjoyable weekend, kid free.

"True. I need to focus on the positive." Rachel let out a breath, loosening the tightness in her chest. "I get to spend the weekend with you, my best friend. And it's been way too long."

"Exactly," Haley agreed.

"But Haley . . ." Rachel gnawed on her fingernail, nearly ruining her new manicure. "Am I totally off base with this whole 'trying to win him over' plan?"

"No," Haley firmly replied, "and I'd tell you the truth. Now stop spiraling." Haley spoke over a loudspeaker announcement in the background. "That's me. I need to board. Keep it together until I get there. Okay?"

Rachel agreed and ended the call.

Tossing her phone back into her purse, Rachel paused, gnawing on a fingernail. Her mom had always taught her to not slouch, but instead to be proud of her tall, long, and lean frame. Somehow it became her mantra, carrying her through her middle school years, when she towered over the boys in her class.

Rachel squared her shoulders, and then, as if on cue, the sliding glass doors to the hotel lobby opened, blasting out refreshing air-conditioned air. The cool air shot a tingle down her spine. When she didn't immediately enter, they slammed shut again. *Come on, you've got this.* Adjusting her purse and luggage, she walked forward. The doors reopened, and she crossed the threshold into the lobby.

A huge banner hung across the middle of the lobby ceiling, greeting her graduating class. Encouraged by the welcoming sign, she smiled. Nostalgia washed over her. A flood of happy memories came back, specifically her high school graduation, held in the banquet room because the high school gym floor had been resurfaced. It was forever ago and yesterday at the same time.

A packed lobby bustled with people as the excitement of happy reunions occurred all around her. Brandon was somewhere in this mass of people. She knew it. Her imagination ran wild with the possible romantic rendezvous. Maybe he would take one look at her and with a dropped jaw say breathlessly, *Where have you been my whole life?* Then she would toss her hair over her shoulder and laugh flirtatiously while she basked in his adoring gaze. Well, certainly, one could dream.

Lost in her little dream world, she wasn't paying attention to her surroundings. A man cut across the path in front of her. She tripped on the wheel of her roller suitcase. Her arms flew forward, and she looked for anything to help her regain her balance.

"Whoa . . ." The man crossing in front of her grabbed onto her, attempting to hold her steady. "Are you okay?"

Her eyes dilated as she scanned his face. "Oh . . . sorry."

Rachel rammed into her roller suitcase, stumbling backwards. Floundering, she gripped tightly to the good-looking man with jet-black hair and green eyes. His blue and green button-down seersucker shirt made his eyes pop. *Whoa. Where had this guy been back in high school?* Her stomach fluttered like a forlorn teenager.

"Ahh—" Rachel attempted to find her footing.

Once both of her feet were on solid ground, she straightened her dress and patted down her hair.

He released his grip, taking a small step back so they were no longer rammed up against one another.

"Thank you." Rachel stammered. "I didn't see you."

He chuckled. "I believe you."

After a long pause, Rachel cleared her throat. "Are you here for the reunion?"

Please say yes. Please say yes. Please say yes.

He ran a hand through his thick locks, then rubbed his jaw before shoving his hand into his pocket. "Yep. I'm here for the reunion, Rachel." He shifted his weight and gave her a once over. "It's good to see you."

It was a miracle. He remembered her. What was his name? Her mind went blank. *Come on, remember him. He remembers you.*

"Yes . . . I'm Rachel." Fidgeting with the handle of her suitcase, Rachel asked, "Did you go to Cloverton?"

"I sure did."

He smiled. A warm, I'll-take-care-of-you-forever smile, settling the weird swimming sensation in her stomach.

"I'm James." James pulled his hand out of his pocket, placing it over his heart. "James Ripley."

Squinting, she slowly repeated, "James Ripley . . ." She gnawed on her bottom lip. "Sorry. It's not ringing a bell."

Rachel suddenly wished she remembered him.

James waved it off. "No worries. It makes sense." He scratched his head, pausing. A loud ruckus interrupted them, and he glanced over his shoulder toward the classmates congregated at the hotel bar. The group quieted down. Shuffling his feet, James finally said, "I wasn't exactly Mr. Popular in high school, but you were in my English class our senior year. I sat right behind you."

"You did?" questioned Rachel.

Why couldn't she remember him? James wasn't easy to forget, at least not now. It must be that time had been good to him.

Rachel dreamed he thought the same about her. Because oh boy, James with his broad shoulders, a chiseled jawline, and dazzling green eyes made her body buzz from merely standing in his presence. *Yes, please.*

James laughed, making her insides turn on themselves.

"Yep." His eyes twinkled with mischievousness. Moving his hands out of his pocket a tad, he looped his thumbs through his belt loops. "I can clearly see I made zero impression on you."

A man walked by and clapped James on the back. He turned, greeting him with a broad smile. As they exchanged a few pleasantries, Rachel tried not to stare as his movements made his hair fall ever so perfectly across his forehead. James introduced the man to Rachel, but she was distracted the entire time, checking James out. James had a rugged, outdoorsy appeal, like he belonged in the back country, chopping wood—shirtless. More heat wiggled its way down her spine. *Easy tiger.* Once the man left, Rachel immediately forgot his name, and James brought his attention back to her.

There was a long, uncomfortable pause. Her skin crawled. Where was her A-game?

James tilted his head. "Sorry, what were we talking about?"

"How I was an idiot not to notice you back in high school," Rachel muttered under her breath.

Smirking, James cocked an eyebrow.

Whoa, wait. You're here for Brandon.

Rachel shook her head, clearing her throat. "Nothing important." She pulled back her shoulders, rediscovering her confidence. "Only about how you remember me, and I simply have a hazy memory of you."

His cheeks tinged pink, making him even more attractive.

"I'm not surprised." James shifted a step closer. "I tried to blend in, to survive the whole arduous four years."

You aren't blending in now.

Her gaze flickered quickly over his perfectly proportioned frame. No way this guy ever blended in.

Finding common ground, Rachel replied. "You and me both."

Trust me.

"Liar," James countered. His nostrils flared. "I have it on good authority that you broke many hearts back in high school."

Her face flushed with heat, spreading down her neck. What hearts? She'd love to know. She spent all of high school chasing down one guy, and one guy only, Brandon Belford. Just the name crossing her psyche made her pulse uptick and sweat slather her brow. And boom—just like that, she was back on the Brandon train. No time to waste on anyone else, right? Not even James. Though she fully admitted, he was a total hottie.

James shuffled his feet, snapping her back to their conversation. "I'm glad I ran into you, Rachel. You look good. *Real* good."

"Yes—the years have treated you well, too." Her hand flew to her mouth, covering it. Rachel's eyes widened. Then she forced her lips into a tight smile. "Will I see you tomorrow at the reunion?"

James straightened his stance. "Yes. I'll see you tomorrow."

"Until tomorrow." Rachel continued past him, brushing his arm on her way to the hotel check-in line.

She shook off the encounter and tried to focus on her original plan: Find Brandon and get him to fall in love with her.

A long line traveled from the front desk to halfway through the lobby. A few familiar people passed by while she waited. Rachel greeted them, chatting, while the line slowly crept forward. During high school, she preferred to stick with her bestie Haley, but Rachel had participated in many extracurricular activities, so she knew most people from her graduating class.

Still, if you had asked her last year if she would attend her ten-year high school reunion, she would've laughed. Then, when Brandon updated his relationship status from married to divorced on social media, Rachel nearly flipped. She didn't need a bigger sign. Her second chance was this weekend. With Brandon.

In high school, Brandon had been *everything*. He knew it, too, and he had used it to his advantage, dating everyone in their graduating class. Well, *practically* everyone, everyone but Rachel. He had spent most of high school ignoring her, except for one night. The encounter still made her stomach all topsy-turvy whenever she thought about it, even though it was years ago.

During a basketball game her senior year, she had nearly peed her pants when he slid into the seat next to her. His friend group happened to be sitting behind her, but the bench was full when Brandon arrived, so he plopped right down in the empty space next to her. The game went into overtime, and his friends left to go to a party while Brandon decided to hang back.

After a few nail-biting plays by their team, the two exchanged high fives when the team scored a three-pointer, giving them the lead. She nearly died, like the very breath in her lungs failed to fill back up. Then Brandon casually asked Rachel about their upcoming physics test. They fell into a conversation, anxious for her and seemingly thoughtless for him. Brandon ended up talking to her for the rest of the game. When the buzzer sounded and the team ran off the court, Rachel expected Brandon to quickly make his exit. Instead, he had *lingered*, walking her out to the parking lot.

When she stopped in front of her car, fiddling with her keys, Rachel bravely met his eyes. Seconds ticked by like an eternity, and Rachel panicked. She knew Brandon was going to kiss her, but she'd had little experience. Only one kiss under the bleachers, when she was sixteen. Sure, Brandon kissed people all the time, for fun, for kicks. What if she messed up? How could she know she was doing it right? Maybe he would be repulsed by her lack of kissing ability.

Rachel moved closer to the car, leaning her back against it. Brandon shifted his weight toward her, moving only inches away. Then he reached out, brushing her hair out of her eyes like a total boss.

But instead of leaning in and encouraging him to continue, Rachel had nervously laughed, averting her glance. A group of loud students meandered toward them, breaking the spell. Brandon jumped back, removing his hand. He mumbled good-bye, nearly running to his car. Swoosh—the moment disappeared as quickly as it had come. High school ended a few weeks later, and their paths didn't cross again before graduation. She missed her chance.

It had eaten her up every day since then. What if she hadn't chickened out? What if she had simply leaned in and kissed him? Maybe they would have ended up together. Maybe. Maybe. Maybe. The not knowing was the worst part. This weekend, she wanted an answer. She hoped to rewrite the past.

Eventually, she made it to the front reception counter and checked in, receiving her room key.

With key and roller suitcase in hand, she headed toward the elevator. It dinged. The doors of the elevator swung open, revealing Brandon. Her insides did a somersault while her heart skidded to a halt. *Breathe, breathe, breathe.* The world began to move in slow motion, like when the music starts to play in a rom-com movie during the meet-cute. But this wasn't a movie. Brandon, in the flesh, stepped off the elevator with a cell phone glued to his ear.

Rachel paused, blinking. She found her voice. "Hey . . . Bran-don." The words were shaky and a tad too loud.

Brandon's gaze found hers. Tilting his head to the side, a look of confusion crossed his face. He furrowed his brows, making the lines on his forehead deepen. He paused, covering the mouthpiece of his phone with his hand. "Do I know you?" Brandon questioned.

Poof. Her shoulders slouched. This couldn't be happening. The man didn't even remember her. They had almost kissed!

"It's Rachel." She tucked her hair behind her ears, forcing herself to stand up straight. Plastering a smile on her face, she pointed at her chest. "Rachel Millson."

His eyes formed tight slits. Brandon gave her a quick once over. A few beats of time passed, which stretched out like infinity. Shaking his head, he finally replied, "Sorry. I don't know you." Brandon took his hand off the mouthpiece, putting it back up to his ear. He briskly brushed past her and spoke into the phone. "Okay, sounds like a plan. Wilson's at seven for drinks. I'll be there." His voice eventually became indistinguishable as he strode across the lobby, all the way outside.

Her face sagged. Brandon didn't even remember her. At all?! Nada. Zero. Zilch. Worse, he gave her the complete brush off. This entire weekend was a mistake. A big one. Colossal. If there had been a cave to crawl into, she would have welcomed the reprieve from this total humiliation.

Knees wobbly, she filed into the elevator with the other guests who had been waiting.

In a depressed daze, miraculously, she made it to her room, where she promptly dumped her stuff by the door and catapulted herself face forward onto the bed. With a face full of pillow, she screamed and pounded the fluffy pillow-top mattress. Tantrum over, she flipped to her back, staring up at the ceiling tiles. Forcing herself to calm down, she breathed in and out, repeatedly, until she managed to drift off to sleep.

A banging at the door awoke her a few hours later. She rose, stumbling across the hotel room toward the door. Groggy, she swiped at her eyes as the knocking continued.

"I'm coming," Rachel shouted as she tripped over her suitcase on the way, almost hitting her chin on the wall. "Hold your horses." She swung open the door, revealing Haley. Rachel squealed, clapping her hands together. "Haley! You made it!"

They hugged.

"I did." Haley broke their embrace. "I'm glad I didn't end up spending the entire weekend in the airport." She filed into the hotel room behind Rachel. "Also, I'm glad we decided to stay in the hotel instead of at our parents' houses. My parents turned the spare room into a TV room."

"I'm glad we're staying here, too," Rachel agreed. "It gives us a better chance of being with everyone. My parents' house is in the middle of a remodel, so they are out of town until Sunday to escape the mess. But I'm going to meet up with my parents and brother after the reunion for dinner, before I head back to New York."

"I'm doing the same." Haley waved a hand. "Did I miss anything?" Raising an eyebrow, she eyed Rachel.

Rachel adjusted her twisted dress, averting her glance. "I think this weekend might've been a mistake," she muttered, following the statement with a loud exhale.

Haley scanned the room, waving off the idea. "Nonsense. I'm out of Boston. And this is the first time in months I'm a free woman without Elsa in tow." She placed her suitcase on the sofa, then plopped herself down on one of the queen beds, wagging a finger in her direction. "You aren't ruining my newfound freedom."

Rachel sat down on the edge of the bed opposite her. "I won't. We'll have fun together, no matter what the weekend holds. It just . . . I already saw Brandon."

"You what?" Haley nearly fell off the bed when her body lunged forward from the news. "Why didn't you text me and tell me?"

"I fell asleep." Rachel shook her head, burying her face in her hands. Her hair cascaded down, covering it. She groaned. "He didn't even remember me." Then she peeked over between her fingers.

Haley waved her hands. "Wait. Wait. Please go back—to the beginning." She spoke slowly, enunciating each word. "I need to hear about the whole interaction from start to finish."

Climbing fully on top of the bed, Rachel settled next to Haley before she said, "I saw him getting off the elevator. I mean, he was walking right toward me. I thought this is it, manna from heaven." She gave Haley a crooked smile. "He was on the phone, but I decided to be brave. I wasn't going to be timid and shy like how I was in high school. I mustered up the courage to say hello. He paused, looked me square in the eyes and said, I quote, 'I don't know you,' then went back to talking on the phone."

Haley sucked in air. "Geez. Harsh. I'm sorry, that totally bites."

Rachel gnawed on the inside of her cheek. "It's the worst."

"He doesn't remember you." Haley squeezed Rachel on the arm. Her voice took on a tad-too-chipper tone. "It doesn't mean this whole thing's a wash. You do have the entire weekend to make something happen. Besides, you're completely different from how you were in high school. Maybe if he is given the chance, Brandon might end up liking what he sees."

She mulled over Haley's comment. Rachel wasn't a person who quit things at the first sign of trouble. If anything, she often became energized from challenging situations. This was a big reason why she excelled as a labor and delivery nurse. She had an ability to quickly regroup. "I did overhear him tell the person on the phone he was going to Wilson's tonight at seven."

Haley slapped her on the knee. "See, you still have a chance." She grinned. Her arms made a wide-open gesture. "I guess this means we're going to Wilson's tonight at seven."

Rachel fiddled with her hands in her lap. "Do you think that's a good idea?"

Swinging her legs over the side of the bed, Haley leaned

forward. "Maybe it is, maybe it isn't." She popped up one shoulder. "But what do you have to lose?"

"Nothing," Rachel muttered.

Except her pride, along with her hopes and dreams.

"That's right. Nothing." Haley glanced at her wristwatch. "We have a whole half hour to get you looking smoking hot. Hopefully, you have some new outfits for me to approve."

"I did go on a bit of a shopping spree." Rachel exhaled, pushing out the tightness trapped inside her chest. "I hope I'm up for this. It's incredibly exhausting to put yourself out there, and I've only begun."

"We came all this way for you to see Brandon, and for you to get a second chance." Haley stood, reaching for her suitcase. "Come on. You need to give this one more good ol' college try or you'll regret it later." She gave her a sideways glance.

Rachel threw up her hands. "You've convinced me." She went and retrieved her suitcase dumped by the door.

Both women changed and freshened up. Once properly primed, and at the fashionably late time of 7:15, Rachel and Haley walked across the hotel lobby and out the sliding glass doors. Luckily, the muggy air had cooled significantly, but gnats danced around in full force. Rachel swatted them away. Wilson's was located a block down Main Street from the hotel.

"Have you seen anyone else we know?" asked Haley as they walked toward the restaurant.

Rachel gripped her clutch tighter. "I've chatted with a few people. But no big standouts." Then she stopped abruptly, Haley nearly tripped over her heels. "Wait. I did run into a guy named James. Ripley?" She squinted as she questioned her memory. "Yes. James Ripley. I didn't remember him, but he remembered me. A real hottie with a body."

Rachel knew she was smirking as she thought about James.

After her run-in with Brandon, she had completely forgotten about James. Ahh, James, sweet baby James.

Haley cocked her head to the side. "James Ripley." She nodded, starting to walk again. A few steps later, she snapped her finger and pointed. "Yes. James Ripley. Dark hair, beautiful green eyes—I think he was in English with us."

"That's him." Rachel's mind wandered back to James. Her stomach did a weird fluttery flip-flop. "I honestly have no recollection of him, which makes no sense to me, because the guy is *gorgeous*." Her voice was overly sing-songy. "I wouldn't mind seeing him again. Of course, that's if things with Brandon don't pan out."

"Without a doubt, but you're keeping your options open. I like it," Haley chuckled. "I always liked James. He was nice, but always kind of kept to himself. Last I heard, he was an attorney, like a big fancy one, in New York City."

"He lives in New York City too," Rachel repeated, mostly for herself. *What were the odds?*

Haley nodded. "I believe so." Then, almost as a second thought, she added, "I always thought he had a crush on you."

"What?" Rachel nearly choked on her own saliva. "You did?"

This was news to her. Rachel hadn't been swimming in dates back in high school. If she had known, she would've welcomed the admiration. But she understood being too reserved to make a move on someone. Look at how she acted around Brandon.

Haley smirked. "James was always trying to be in our study group. I knew he didn't like me, because he always turned bright red whenever he was around you."

Rachel's eyes widened. "I made someone turn red . . . I'm flattered." How had she never noticed? "Geez, was I completely dense that I didn't notice a cute boy like James looking my way?" She made a tsk sound with her tongue. "I blame Brandon. He messed with my head."

"What can you say?" Haley elbowed her. "You've only had eyes for one guy. And—still do."

Rachel shrugged. "Unfortunately, yes."

"Hey, you're giving destiny one last chance to make something happen." Haley looped her arm through Rachel's. "You might as well see this thing all the way through."

CHAPTER TWO

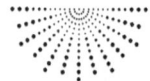

At one of the high-top tables near the bar at Wilson's, James visited with his best friend, Ryan. Surrounded by several of his former classmates, the place had a party vibe. The restaurant pulsated with energy, and James couldn't help but feel invigorated by the atmosphere. Surely, with such a large crowd, Rachel would make an appearance at some point. One could hope. Rachel Millson. He let out a long breath while he remembered the very sight of her had knocked the wind right out of him. A flood of memories came drifting back, especially all those flirtatious exchanges they had shared during English class. Or at least that was how he remembered it. Ten years . . . Rachel still had the most beautiful long blonde hair and blue eyes. *Okay, okay, down boy.*

It wasn't a surprise Rachel didn't remember him. Most didn't. All through high school, he used his weekends to study and catch up on assignments. His home life had been awful, and he only had one ticket out of Cloverton—good grades. Those four years passed painfully slowly while he bided his time until he could fly the coop. On the day of his graduation, he booked a one-way bus ticket—he couldn't afford a plane ticket—to New York City. With everything he owned stuffed into a used duffle bag or tucked into his pocket, including his entire life savings he had managed to scrape together from delivering pizzas, James hoped New York University would be all he dreamed it to be.

When the bus pulled away from the station, James immediately breathed lighter than he had in years. As the shops of Main Street left his view, he promised himself he would never return. Not for anything or anyone. And he meant it. Cloverton encapsulated years of bad experiences. Nobody cared about him in that little town, so he refused to grace it with his presence ever again. At least that had been the plan.

The choice to come to his high school ten-year reunion had been a last-minute decision, though Ryan had been begging him for weeks to attend with him. Without warning, the case he had been buried under as a corporate attorney had crashed and burned, leaving him with the weekend wide open. A true rarity. When he scanned the RSVP list looking for Rachel's name, he smiled when he saw her on the list. Presented with the unexpected chance to reconnect and rewrite the past, he called up Ryan and told him he'd go.

As the restaurant inched toward its capacity, the air became hot and stifling. James tugged at the collar of his blue seersucker shirt, wishing the staff would crank up the air conditioning. Clearly, they hadn't planned on such a large and boisterous crowd this weekend.

Ryan nudged him with his elbow, interrupting his scattered thoughts.

Ryan spoke loudly over the noise. "Can you believe how many people came?"

James chuckled. "Nope—and I don't know most of these people." Craning his neck, he glanced around the room full of people. Half he recognized, and the other he couldn't pick out of a lineup. "Suddenly, I'm acutely aware of how little I did in high school, besides study."

"But look at you now . . ." Ryan made a wide gesture with his arm. "All your hard work has paid off. You're a powerful attorney. Once women here find out, they'll be fighting each other for a chance to get their claws into you."

Rolling his eyes, James took a sip of his drink. "I appreciate your enthusiasm, but I seriously doubt that."

If only it worked that way. If only dating was easy like a Sunday morning. But James knew the opposite to be true. His job often became a deterrent for women rather than a plus. With rarely any extra time to socialize, let alone date, James's long trail of unsuccessful relationships was filled with girlfriends annoyed with his work hours and countless distractions. The entire dating process became arduous and unappealing years ago. Marriage, or even a relationship, might not be in the cards for him. And that thought depressed him more than anything.

With a quick scan around the room, James searched for Rachel. Unable to spot her, James reverted his attention back to Ryan. He asked Ryan a few investment questions. Ryan lived in New York City, too, and worked as a trader on Wall Street. Both had hectic schedules that were opposite from each other, which made hanging out with one another nearly impossible. Ryan got up before sunrise, while James often worked late into the night. This weekend was a welcome respite from his normal day-to-day grind.

Deep in conversation, James jolted as a server dropped a handful of dishes right beside him. Both stopped talking, waiting for the mess to be cleaned up. James glanced around the restaurant. He was surprised by how many more people had arrived. Before they returned to their conversation, a loud commotion sounded near the entrance. James shifted, peering in the direction of the ruckus. His stomach lurched. The sleazy, no-good guy, Brandon Belford entered.

Just seeing the guy in the flesh made his jaw tighten and hands form into fists. Man, James hated him. Even after all these years, James found it hard to forget how Brandon had made his life miserable in high school. James had been the constant butt of Brandon's jokes. Brandon had loved to point out and make fun of his worn clothes and ratty shoes.

Joke was on him. James became an attorney at one of the most elite firms in New York, and he was right on track to make partner at the firm. These days, he could afford the nicest clothes and shoes. And unlike Brandon, James never made fun of anyone, ever. If anything, he tried his best to be generous and kind. What had Brandon done with his life? Nothing. Except make an endless string of dumb decisions. The guy hadn't changed one bit. Once a jerk, always a jerk.

Last James had heard, Brandon had been slapped with divorce papers when his wife had caught him cheating. Surprise, surprise. A real jaw-dropping shocker. Not. Brandon was a self-proclaimed womanizer. But with the warm welcome he received from the women upon his entrance to Wilson's here tonight, apparently nobody cared about his colorful past. Cloverton never changed, nor did these people. Here, all they valued was the past.

James gripped his glass tightly. A pinch between his shoulder blades spread pain down his back. He forced himself to breathe, to fight against the feelings of unresolved anger bubbling up in his chest. Brandon and guys like him would always exist. Who cares? Best of luck to him, because James only had his eye on one woman: Rachel. He doubted Brandon even knew her or remembered her the way he did.

Brandon made his way through the restaurant, heading toward where they sat. He hugged and slapped the backs of practically every person he walked by, inching closer to James and Ryan.

His neck stiffened. James rolled it from side to side to loosen it up. Taking a sip of his drink, he muttered to Ryan, "Can you believe that guy?" His jaw tightened.

Ryan craned his neck above the heads of those standing up.

"Brandon Belford." He swung back around, leaning forward. "Man, I can't stand him either." He rolled his eyes while he played with his drink straw. "He's the worst. If I remember correctly, he made your life miserable in high school."

James groaned. "Please, don't remind me." He ran his hands back and forth over the top of his khakis. "I hoped he wouldn't show up."

Shifting, Ryan took another glance in the direction of Brandon before he straightened himself. He nudged James with his shoulder.

"Remember, Brandon doesn't have anything going for him. His life is a complete train wreck. Don't let him get to you." Ryan gazed out across the crowded restaurant, sipping on a drink. He set it back down, folding his hands on the tabletop. "He isn't worth it. The guy is a total loser. You have done way more with your life than he has."

James narrowed his eyes, wishing for the anger to pass. "I know, but seeing him . . ." He pushed up the sleeves of his shirt as the bad memories of high school came roaring back with a vengeance. The ones he had spent the last ten years trying to forget. Awful experiences, right there, taunting him, refusing to be forgotten. "I'm regretting my decision to come." He swallowed a sip of his drink, gulping the torture of the past back down.

"For real, don't give him another thought." Ryan grabbed a few nuts from the bowl on the table, popping them into his mouth. "I doubt he'll even remember what a total jerk he was to you. A guy like that doesn't remember all the horrible things he has done. He conveniently forgets," Ryan scoffed.

"You're probably right." James chewed on the end of his straw. Here he was, a grown man, worried about some guy who wouldn't even remember him. *Forget about him. You came here for Rachel. Drop it.*

Brandon arrived at the high-top tables, mingling and chatting with those in that section. James kept his eyes forward, avoiding interaction. But after a few minutes, Brandon passed by, and James made the mistake of looking directly at him.

Moving closer, Brandon took a sip of his drink and initiated a conversation. "You two look familiar. Did you go to Cloverton High, too?" He put his free hand into the pocket of his slacks.

James's shoulders tightened, and he forced himself to straighten his back, and not shrink into himself.

Ryan cleared his throat. "Yep. We went to high school with you, *Brandon*." His tone was a tad sharp.

Brandon smirked, his eyes brightening. "You guys remember me?" Clearly ignoring Ryan's tone, he oozed annoying confidence. Nothing had changed. "Of course you do. I was the *star* football player and prom king." He took another sip of his drink, while he gave numerous nods to those who caught his eyes.

James gritted his teeth, reminding himself to be gracious. "Yes, Brandon. You were everything back then." He wanted to add, *look at you now, a used car salesman. Well done.* But he managed to refrain from flinging insults.

With his glance elsewhere, Brandon asked, "What were your names again?"

Ryan pointed to his chest. "Ryan Holt." Then he pointed with his thumb toward James. "This is James Ripley."

Brandon glanced above their heads, taking in the crowd. Shifting, he didn't answer for a long time. Finally, he gave a head nod to someone on the other side of the room. After a patronizing pat on Ryan's back, Brandon moved away from them.

Over his shoulder, Brandon replied, "Yeah, I don't remember you guys. Bye." Then he walked off, giving a wink to a group of gawking women as he passed by them, and beelined for the crowd of former cheerleaders.

Once out of earshot, James stopped watching Brandon surf his way through the restaurant. He turned back to Ryan and said, "He hasn't learned *anything* in the past ten years." James shook his head. "He's the same douche bag."

Ryan finished the rest of his drink. "Agreed." He slid out of his chair, slapping James on the back. "Forget about Brandon. Let's go mingle."

He groaned. Mingle. A root canal at the dentist sounded more appealing. Then, almost as if on cue, Rachel walked in with Haley. She had changed into a formfitting, lacy green dress. Heat wiggled all the way down to his gut. His palms started to sweat.

Sliding out of his seat, James stood. He straightened his back. "Fine, let's do it. But you know me, I'm awkward at these types of things. I plan on following you around and letting you introduce me to everyone."

Ryan chuckled, then smirked. "I'm happy to oblige." He scanned the crowd. "Do you see anyone you recognize?"

"Nah. Umm . . ." James gazed over at Rachel on the far side of the restaurant. She was still near the entrance. He wanted to talk to her, but he wasn't ready. Not yet. Instead, he pointed in the direction of a group of people he recognized from a few of their science classes. "I believe we know them."

Ryan's brow furrowed, then loosened. "Ahh, yes, Mr. Crook-shank's chemistry class." Ryan moved toward them.

James followed behind him, speaking over the crowd. "Mr. Crookshank . . . I haven't thought about him in years. I wonder if he's still teaching."

Ryan shrugged. "No idea."

Then they joined in a conversation with the classmates James had recognized.

From the corner of his eye, James tracked Rachel, watching her gracefully glide through the crowd. Her blonde hair was bouncy, fluttering around her shoulders as she moved through the restaurant. She was gorgeous, making it near impossible for him to pay attention to the conversation with his classmates. Somehow, he needed to find a way to talk to Rachel again. His entire being ached to be near her.

Rachel and Haley continued through the crowd. James

tracked them, watching as Rachel moved swiftly from one end of the room toward the other. People tried to engage her in conversation, but she pressed forward through the crowd, obviously steering for someone. James wondered at the object of her desire. Then, after tracking Rachel's line of vision, James landed squarely on Brandon Belford. His stomach plummeted. He wanted to be wrong.

Surely Rachel was different . . . but as she inched closer toward Brandon, James knew. He outwardly groaned as his insides twisted. Running a hand down the length of his face, James wished for the sinking feeling in his stomach to leave him. Diverting his attention away from Rachel, he made himself engage in the conversation playing out in front of him. His being was numb as his dreams of Rachel withered away with the muggy air through the opened side doors.

Against his will, James peered over a few times as he watched Rachel speak to Brandon. Within moments, she was laughing and leaning in closer to him. Her body language clearly testified to her interest in him. He almost became unhinged when she did one of those cute hair flipping things. Defeated, he refused to look in her direction for ten whole minutes, which proved to be excruciatingly painful. When James finally allowed himself to glance over at Rachel, she and Haley were alone.

Abruptly, James interrupted the conversation with the group. "Excuse me." He held up his hand. "I'm so sorry to interrupt. It was great seeing you all." He shifted toward Ryan, tilting his head toward him. "Ryan, can I speak with you for a moment?"

Before he even had time to reply, James tugged Ryan by the elbow, leading him away from the group.

Ryan raised an eyebrow but complied. He hissed above the loud room, "What's gotten into you?"

James said over his shoulder, peering back toward Ryan. "I saw someone I want to talk to." He ducked and dived through the throngs of former classmates. Ryan trailed along behind him. "Please, just go with it."

"This better be good," Ryan muttered. "I thought two of those women were cute."

James paused for a moment, making eye contact with Ryan. "Hey, I need you to be my wingman for a minute." He tugged at his shirt collar.

"Wingman," Ryan chuckled. His eyes brightened as his demeanor softened. "Why didn't you just say so? I thought you'd never ask."

James squared his shoulders, making the tension in his shoulders loosen. He continued his way toward Rachel and Haley. *What are you doing? What's the plan, Einstein?* James questioned himself. Honestly, his boldness surprised him. But seeing Brandon lit a fire under him. Brandon always won. At everything. This time he wasn't winning Rachel over too, not if he had anything to do with it. Within a few feet of them, Rachel abruptly turned, stepping right into him. Another stroke of good luck.

"Whoa . . ." James reached out, steadying Rachel with both of his hands. He held onto her forearms while she regained her balance. "Be careful. It's crowded here. Almost like a mosh pit at a concert."

Smooth, real smooth.

Her eyes dilated while her cheeks reddened. Dang, she looked cute.

"I'm *so* sorry." Rachel darted her glance away while shuffling her feet to regain her balance. "It seems I've run into you yet again." She smiled meekly. Then she exchanged a look with Haley.

"I wish you'd do it more." James released his grip on her forearms, taking a step back. He tugged at his shirt collar. Another person pressed against him, almost shoving him back against Rachel's body. He motioned with his arm. "Here, let's move out of the crossfire."

James led Rachel and Haley further away from the crowd to the back corner of the restaurant.

Rachel leaned her back against the wall. The overly loud sound of old friends reconnecting in the enclosed space went down a notch, enough for him to hear her ask, "James, who's your friend?" She peered over his shoulder at where Ryan stood.

"Ahh," James moved out of the way, opening the circle to Ryan. With a hand on his chest, he said, "Pardon me. I'm being rude."

James introduced Ryan, and Haley introduced herself, too.

Rachel tilted her head to the side as she examined Ryan's face. Her hands fiddled with her clutch purse. "Yes . . . okay . . . I've got a cloudy recollection of you two." She wagged her finger at them.

Haley smiled. "I remember you both fondly," she added.

James pushed a shaky hand through his hair, his heart rate still elevated. "If I remember correctly, you two were joined at the hip in high school."

The ladies locked eyes with one another and laughed.

Rachel smirked. "Guilty as charged."

The four continued to talk, catching up for a minute. James couldn't believe his luck. Rachel was warming up to him.

Casually, James leaned against the wall, crossing his ankles. "Hey, do you remember senior year, when the class president stole the principal's car and parked it on the football field?"

"Oh, do I," Rachel laughed. "I remember him bragging about his plan to pull it off, but nobody, me included, believed he would do it."

Haley piped in. "I remember the principal announced on the loudspeaker whoever was involved wouldn't walk at graduation."

"Luckily, nobody ratted him out," added James.

"How about you?" Rachel asked. "Did you pull off any pranks?"

"Me?" James pointed at his chest, then shook his head. "Hardly. I think the most dangerous thing I ever did as a teenager was sneak into a double feature at the drive-in by hiding in the trunk."

Ryan chuckled. "I completely forgot about that."

After some more chitchat about their daring high school memories, someone called out Rachel's name with a shriek.

All four of them shifted and peered in the direction of the voice.

Rachel clapped her hands together as the woman moved closer to them. "That's Trisha." She grabbed onto Haley's arm, tugging her toward Trisha. "If you'll excuse us . . ."

Before James had time to reply, they left.

His shoulders slumped. James thought the conversation had been going well with Rachel. He had even picked up a slight flirty vibe, but now he was beginning to think it was all wishful thinking on his end.

Ryan and James bumped into a few more classmates, catching up. James tried to brush off his encounter with Rachel, but his mind was fixated on her and analyzing their conversation. After enduring a couple more hours of small talk, James was itching to leave.

Sweat dripped down his back, and James swiped at the moisture on his brow. "Do you want to get out of here?" he asked Ryan.

Ryan nodded, following James to the exit. Once outside, the cool, refreshing night air hit James's skin. James sighed, grateful to be out of the hot and crowded restaurant. Noise from the restaurant flowed out of the opened doors. But as they walked toward the hotel, Wilson's party noise became dimmer and dimmer. Though it was dark, the sparkling stars lit the sky. If James didn't remember he was in Cloverton, he might have enjoyed the sight more. Walking, James shoved his hands into his pockets, wondering again why he had returned to this town he hated.

"I can see you still have a thing for Rachel." Ryan broke the silence, peering over at him.

James gritted his teeth. "Is it that obvious?" His shoulders slumped.

"Yes." Ryan chuckled, then nudged him with his elbow. "But don't worry, you were acting completely normal. It's only, I'm your best friend, and I know you've had it bad for her," he gave him a sideways glance, "since forever."

"Unfortunately, yes." James pulled a hand out of his pocket, rubbing the stubble on his jaw. "I'm her forever admirer. I'm afraid I'll only ever be that."

Acknowledging his worst fear out loud only made the situation even more miserable. Rachel liked Brandon. James liked Rachel. But nobody liked James. Boom. Mic drop.

"You can't give up now." Ryan's voice rose an octave. "You never know how these things will play out."

James tried not to feel hopeless. He wanted Ryan's words to buoy up his spirit, but his ego was crumbling. A heart could only take so much rejection.

"I don't know . . ." James paused, rubbing his hand across the back of his neck. Then he shook his head. "She doesn't seem the least bit interested in me."

Ryan raised an eyebrow. "Come on, you talked to her for what, like, two minutes?" The hotel peeked up at the top of the hill. Ryan slowed his pace. "You still have the entire weekend to help her see what a fantastic catch you happen to be."

James scoffed. "I'm not a catch, not by a long shot." Dragging his feet, James wanted to shrug off the thousand things stacked against him, but he couldn't anymore. "I—" He stammered. "I come from a broken home. I have zero contact with any family members. That isn't exactly a huge selling feature. I work long, odd hours. If anything, women look at me and think, *Uh no. That one has too many issues. I'm out.*"

Ryan didn't respond immediately. He swung his gaze from James back to the hotel. Finally, Ryan cleared his throat. "I know you feel insecure in some ways." He made a hand gesture toward his chest. "I get it. Trust me. But family aside, you've made something out of your life, despite your less-than-ideal home. You're a high-powered attorney, raking in the dough. Lead with that." Ryan smirked. His voice became more animated. "If I were you, I'd be dropping that intel whenever I could. You. Are. A. Catch."

James gave Ryan a double take, then chuckled. The tightness in his chest dissipated. Ryan always had an ability to buoy him up. Out of everyone in the whole world, he was the closest thing he had to family. Ryan had witnessed firsthand his rocky past with love. Especially when some of his past broken relationships had led him to spiral into despair.

"I saw her beeline for Brandon when she arrived," James countered, shoving his hand through his hair. "I can't compete against him."

Ryan shook his head. "Nah. Don't worry about him. Just give it time. Brandon is Brandon. She'll figure out soon enough what a jerk he can be. When Rachel comes to her senses, you can be there to help her forget about him."

"Maybe," James added, ready for the conversation about Rachel to be over. Then he cocked an eyebrow. "How about you? Are you hoping to reconnect with anyone?"

"Nobody in particular," Ryan smirked. His eyes twinkled with mischievousness. "But the weekend is young. I've still got plenty of time to make a connection with someone."

James laughed. "This is true. You and your ladies."

The two friends joked the entire way back to the hotel. The weekend was young, and James still had hope.

CHAPTER THREE

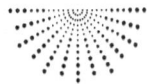

Rachel's heart sank as she leaned her back against the wall of the crowded Wilson's. On the other side of the room, Brandon stood, laughing and talking with a group of beautiful women. The former popular girls of high school. *Typical. A tired cliché.*

Chewing on the end of her straw, she compelled herself to peel her glance away. Forcing herself to finish up her drink, Rachel placed the empty glass on the top of one of the high tables. The steady, pulsating beat of loud conversations reached an excruciating level, making her temples throb. Hot and muggy, Rachel had enough of watching women drool all over Brandon. Never mind that she happened to be one of them too.

Tilting her head toward Haley, Rachel asked in a near-shout, "You want to get out of here?" Her voice was nearly swallowed up.

Haley took a sip of her drink, leaning in closer to Rachel. "What?" She cupped her ear.

Rachel yelled into Haley's cupped ear. "Are you ready to leave?"

Haley eagerly nodded. "Yes. Please."

The two swam through the sea of people. Rachel tried with all of her might not to glance over her shoulder at Brandon as she passed him by. She failed. He laughed and touched the shoulder of a woman with perfectly coiffed hair. Her stomach plummeted. She cared. Too much. Clearly, he wasn't interested in her. Sure, she had spent ten years pining over a guy who didn't even remember her. But why couldn't she let him go? The question whirled around her head, making her mind fuzzy. Brandon impaired her judgement. Period. When he was in a room, it was like she had this gravitational pull to be near him.

Now she regretted how she had treated James. He was cute and fun to be around. But no, Rachel managed to mess that up, too. She hadn't meant to cut off the conversation when she saw her friend, Trisha, but Rachel had been overjoyed to see her. Then by the time she'd realized how much time had passed, and how incredibly rudely she'd had acted, James had already left. So, there you go. Rachel had fried her chances with not one, but two different men in one night.

If only this was the first time she had crashed and burned. Unfortunately, it was a common storyline in her life. Some of it was due to her inability to pick out the sheep from the wolves, and partly because she fell easily and gave too much. Many times, the relationships were one sided, with her doing all the loving and the guy doing all the taking. Rachel hoped this weekend would be the answer to her lackluster love life, but now she was only discouraged.

On a mission, Rachel moved toward the exit with tunnel vision. Haley trailed a few feet behind her. Once they left the restaurant, the tangy night air hit her skin. Rachel sighed with relief. Immediately, as the smell of dewy grass filled her lungs, the tightness in between her shoulders dissipated. A clear night sky full of twinkling stars danced behind the soft glow of the street-lamps. As the noise from the restaurant faded away, Rachel heard the crickets chirping. Quiet and blissful serenity enveloped Rachel as she wandered with Haley down Main Street. Rachel remembered why people loved Cloverton: small town, bigger heart.

In NYC, the stars were indistinguishable, only a big ole moon up there against the bright lights of the city. The stark contrast made her long for home. Maybe it was time to move back? Her parents were getting older. Being back in Cloverton, something within her was shifting, causing her perspective to change. Maybe a quieter and less noisy life would be better? Though the thought brought her no peace. Being a labor and delivery nurse, she didn't know what her job prospects would be. The dinky local hospital only had a few nurses in labor and delivery.

When she made the big move to NYC after she graduated from college, Rachel had been longing for an adventure. The boundaries of Cloverton edged too close to her, making her practically suffocate. Itching to break away and start a life of her own, NYC had everything she wanted and more. Of course, it was crowded and overpriced, the subway smelled like urine, and weird sewer smells blew around in the air. But after only a week in NYC, Rachel had thought, yep this is my place. NYC. This is me. This is home.

A second thought popped into her head. Did James really live in NYC like Haley suspected? It was embarrassing she hadn't asked. Instead their conversation had been on random high school happenings and local town news. It was a huge oversight. Wow, a major failure.

Slowly, Rachel exhaled, swiping a layer of sweat from her brow. "It's quite pleasant here in the evening, isn't it?"

The feeling of nostalgia washed back over her like high tide. Nostalgia for a life she had lived back then, and not necessarily for the one she had now. Conveniently, she once again forgot all the reasons she had left.

Haley rolled her eyes. "What's gotten into you?" She cocked an eyebrow. "Miss 'I'm too good for my hometown.'"

Rachel whacked her playfully on the arm. "I never said I was too good to live here."

"You didn't have to . . ." Haley's voice trailed off as she halted in place. She pulled her glance from her to the sidewalk.

Rachel popped a hip, resting her hand on it. "Out with it, Haley. I know you have more to say than that."

"I'm beginning to see you have a *very* foggy memory of what you were like back in high school." Haley shook her head. "All you ever talked about was how much you hated Cloverton. You hated the people. The small minds. The lack of anything to do on the weekends. You said the minute you could move away, you would. And you did." She shrugged, dropping her hands to her sides. "So, I figured you left because you believed this place wasn't enough."

"It wasn't that . . ." Rachel wondered how to best explain the pent-up feelings trapped inside of her. "I only needed a little bit of space from my parents." She exhaled, gnawing on her fingernail. "Do you remember how my parents hovered over me in high school? Or how I was always living in the shadow of my overly popular, golden boy of a brother?"

"Yes," Haley nodded, "I remember." Her voice trailed off, and she started walking again. The steady tapping of their feet hitting the pavement filled the gap between them. Then, finally, Haley added, "You really do come alive in NYC. I see why you like it there. But now, after being back here . . . would you ever return to Cloverton? You know, to live?"

Rachel shrugged. "Maybe." Who knew what the future held, but suddenly she wasn't completely opposed to the idea. "I never liked the idea, but now maybe it wouldn't be so bad."

"Wow. Wow." Haley made a mind blown expression with her hands. "I'm shocked. If anything, I think you're ready for a change." Haley elbowed her. "Maybe that change will be finding a hot boyfriend who's worth a move."

"Ha. Ha. Let's not get ahead of ourselves. I clearly have zero chance with Brandon." She shook her head, throwing up her hands. "And he's the entire reason I came."

"Hey." Haley made a pouting face. "What am I? Chopped liver?"

Rachel looped her arm around Haley's elbow. "No, of course not." She waved it off. "I'm sorry, that came out all wrong."

"I know," Haley smirked. "I'm only teasing you, but really, we get to spend the entire weekend together. Let's try to make the most of it. Even if it means the whole Brandon thing is a total flop."

"Agreed," Rachel smiled.

"Don't hate me . . ." Haley gave her a sideways glance, clearing her throat. "But will you forget about Brandon? He's a total jerk. He hasn't changed a bit. Open your mind to some other options."

Rachel bit down on her lip. She was probably right, but for whatever reason, she still wanted Brandon to look her way.

"He was kind of a jerk, wasn't he?" Rachel questioned. Though the words were far from the feelings still rattling around inside of her.

Haley nodded. "Let him go," she said the words slowly. "What about James? He's *cute*." Her voice rose an octave, and a slow smirk crossed her face.

"James?" It came out like a question, though James had been running rampant through her mind all evening.

Thinking about James and his dark hair and stunning green eyes made her stomach pool with warmth. A hazy recollection of him in high school came back, and she smiled to herself. James hadn't been a jerk in high school. And he wasn't one now. In fact, James was the exact opposite: kind, thoughtful, and respectful. He *listened*.

"Yes, James. He's cute, and clearly, he's interested in you. Give him a chance," Haley encouraged her. "You never know what it could lead to."

"Nothing." Deadpan, Rachel said, "It could lead to nothing."

She knew the whole thing had disaster and disappointment written all over it. Yeah, James was good-looking and genuine. But what happened after this weekend was over? "I only came for one guy. And if I can't have Brandon, then I plan on hanging out with you. Then when this weekend is over, I can go home and move on with my life. A life which might require me adopting a bunch of cats."

"Ahh. Come on Rachel." Haley tsked. "Don't be such a downer. It's not that *dire*."

The hotel peeked out at the top of the hill. Step in step, they walked the remaining few yards. Arriving in front of the hotel, the sliding glass doors swung open, and a gentle wave of cool air conditioning washed over them.

"It feels dire." Rachel's shoulders dropped as she stepped through the glass doors into the blissful comfort of the hotel lobby. "If I know anything, it's not to get my hopes up when it comes to love."

Haley shook the top of her blouse with her hand, allowing the cool air to soothe her sweaty chest. "Don't ever give up on finding love. It always finds you when you least expect it. That's what happened to me."

Rachel rolled her eyes. "Okay, Dr. Phil." She was over discussing her love life. "Enough about this." She waved her hands. "Let's go up to our room to change and watch a movie. We can raid the mini fridge. My treat."

"Sounds like my kind of night," Haley laughed. They continued toward the elevator. "What's the plan for tomorrow?"

Rachel hit the elevator call button. "I'll have to check the itinerary, but I think there's a breakfast followed by a hike." She watched the number above the elevator slowly change floors. "Then the main dinner tomorrow night."

"As long as I get to sleep in tomorrow." Haley yawned, covering her mouth with her hand. "I'm sleep deprived, and I want one good night's sleep. If I get that, then this entire weekend was worth it."

"I'm with you." A ping sounded, and the elevator doors opened. Rachel placed her hand over the elevator door to give Haley time to enter before she hit the correct floor button. "Sleep before food. We can skip breakfast and make it to the hike."

The elevator jolted up. Rachel wondered what the weekend held for her because it certainly wasn't Brandon.

Scanning the banquet hall, which was all set up for breakfast, James attempted to spot Rachel. There was no sign of her. *Bummer.* He let out a long, shaky breath.

Ryan, beside him, asked, "Should we go see what they have to eat?"

Distracted, James simply replied, "Sure."

They walked to the buffet table, taking their place at the end, behind a bunch of their fellow alumni. They slowly inched forward. Once at the front of the queue, each grabbed a paper plate and utensils. James loaded up his plate with eggs, potatoes, and ham. Then he grabbed a glass of orange juice. He waited for Ryan to finish gathering his food.

With food in hand, James skimmed the room for Rachel while he asked, "Where do you want to sit?"

Ryan adjusted his plate and cup in hand, then he nudged his head in the direction of a half empty table on the other side of the room. "How about that table?" He looked back at James for confirmation.

James didn't spot Rachel, so he nodded. "Great. I'll follow you."

Ryan crossed the room. James followed behind.

James and Ryan arrived at the table where three women seated. The women looked up at them in unison and stopped eating. Flashing one of his award-winning smiles, Ryan asked, "Mind if we join you?"

James tracked one of the women as she eyed Ryan up and down with interest. She eagerly responded in a part sing-song voice, "Please do."

She scooted her chair closer to the one Ryan slipped into.

"Thanks," replied Ryan as he set his food down in front of himself.

James sat down next to Ryan and tried his best to smile at the three women eyeing the men, waiting for them to initiate conversation. When they didn't, James and Ryan both introduced themselves, the women did the same.

Chloe, the woman who seemed interested in Ryan, glanced at James, and added while pointing at him, "I sat next to you in chemistry our junior year."

James re-examined her face. "Yes, I remember you." He smiled and speared his eggs with his fork. "Ryan was in that class, too." He took a bite.

Chloe leaned forward, cradling her chin with her hand. "Oh . . ." She wistfully sighed. "He sure was, wasn't he. How could I forget?" She winked.

Ryan cleared his throat, staring down at his plate of food. Picking up his fork, Ryan speared some of his eggs. James couldn't tell if Ryan was interested in Chloe or not, but his cheeks tinged a slight pink.

"Yes . . . Chloe. It's nice to see you again." Ryan glanced at the other two women at the table. "And both of you, too." Ryan took a bite of his eggs.

Nodding, the other women went back to eating. Their heads tilted close to one another as they continued a private conversation. James clocked their occupied ring fingers. They weren't interested in having a group chat.

Chloe had a bare ring finger. Her body language showed she was more than ready to change that.

Leaning practically close enough to sit on Ryan's lap, Chloe said, "So, how have the last ten years treated you, *Ryan?*"

Ryan nearly choked on his scrambled eggs. He swallowed, washing it down with some juice. He fiddled with his napkin in his lap. "I can't complain. I live in New York City." Ryan pointed with his thumb toward James. "James does too, but he's an attorney, and I'm a trader on Wall Street."

"Fascinating," Chloe replied while moistening her lips, "a trader on wall street." She whistled.

Ryan's cheeks reddened. "It's not that impressive." He shrugged.

"It is to me," replied Chloe.

Then Chloe went on to completely ignore James, while grilling Ryan about every little aspect of his life over the past ten years. Fine by him. James ate the rest of his meal, half listening to the conversation playing out between Chloe and Ryan, half wishing Rachel would come so he could ditch them and talk to her. But after constantly clocking the entrance, he failed to spot Rachel.

As James finished up his breakfast, he finally saw Rachel enter the banquet room with Haley in tow. The very air in his lungs caught, making it hard for him to breathe normally. Rachel looked amazing, even better than the night before. Today she was dressed in slim-fitting black leggings and a tank top. Her hair was pulled up into a messy knot. His throat grew tight, and his temples pulsated.

James glanced at his watch. According to the itinerary he had been given, the hike would begin any minute. *Now or never. Go Time.* He gathered his trash and abruptly excused himself from Ryan and Chloe. The other two women had left minutes before, without any word to them.

With urgency, James strode across the banquet hall toward Rachel. Luckily, Rachel and Haley lingered directly next to the trash can. His heart nearly in his throat, he approached them, forcing his spiraling wheel of anxiety away. He tossed his trash into the garbage can.

"Hey you two." James shuffled his feet, forcing a smile. His voice was a tad wobbly. He hoped his nervousness wasn't as noticeable to them. "Together as always."

Cringe. Why was he acting like a babbling fool? Man, he had zero game. Calm down. Calm. Down.

Hands shaky, James forced them into his pockets to conceal them.

Rachel smirked, making her eyes twinkle. "You caught us," she stated.

"Guilty," replied Haley.

Then Haley and Rachel exchanged a look. James couldn't read what acknowledgement passed between them. Silence followed, making his skin crawl. *Do something. Say anything. ANYTHING!*

With only one Hail Mary pass in his playbook, James searched his pocket, pulling out a five-dollar bill. "Here's the five bucks I owe you." He held it out to Rachel.

With a confused face, Rachel stared at him, then glanced down at the five dollars. "Did I miss something? Why do you owe me five bucks?" She tilted her head, making her chin jut out.

James shook the bill again. "I owe you five bucks. Here, take it."

He placed it into her hand. His fingers lingered a smidge too long on hers.

"You don't owe me anything." Rachel attempted to give it back. "I'm sure you've confused me with someone else."

James grinned, hoping this whole thing didn't fall flat. "Nah, it was you. I remember." He cleared his throat, collecting himself. Finding his confidence once more, James continued. "Senior year, you wrote in my yearbook. 'I bet you'll be a lawyer. You owe me five bucks if you end up becoming one.'"

"Okay . . ." Rachel forced a laugh, shoving the bill into the side pocket of her leggings. She crossed her arms. Her gaze skidded over him. "Now, why would I ever write that in your yearbook?" Her demeanor softened a smidge.

James ran a hand through his hair. "Remember mock trial? In English class?"

The whole project had been a dream for him. Somehow, he had finagled his way into being teamed up with Rachel and Haley and another kid he doesn't remember. For weeks, he got to work in proximity to Rachel. Being around her had only solidified his complete fascination with her. He remembered those weeks way more than he should.

"Yeah." Rachel blinked. "I remember mock trial."

Haley piped up, snapping, then pointing. "That's right, we were all on the same team."

Rachel's eyes slid over him, making his skin tingly like a sunburn. "I remember you now." She smiled, tilting her head to the side. "You were good at doing cross examinations. I remember being really impressed. It was because of you that we all received an A on the project."

Grinning, James held his arms open in a huge gesture. "Success." His voice rang a tad too loud.

The tightness in his chest dissipated. His heart no longer thundered. Finally, he had managed to make a connection with Rachel. Progress.

Haley snickered. Rachel giggled, making her perfectly intoxicating. He remembered all over again how her laugh made everything seem right in the world. Making Rachel laugh was something he lived off for *years* in high school. Rachel had been his glimmer of hope through the treacherous years of his adolescence. Single handedly, she managed to cast a spell so fierce, he was still living under it.

Once the laughing settled down, Rachel stated, "So, you became a lawyer." She locked eyes with him, making a tingle swoop down his spine. "You're impressing me all over again."

James squared his shoulders. "Thanks. I did . . . become a lawyer."

Rachel pushed a few loose strands of hair behind her ear. She inched a tad closer to him. "So, mister big shot lawyer, where do you live now?" Her eyes twinkled.

James glanced between Rachel and Haley. "I live in New York City."

Smirking, Haley nudged Rachel with her elbow. "I was right. Would you look at that? So does Rachel."

His jaw dropped. Rachel lived in NYC too. What were the odds? How long had she been there? More questions clicked through his mind like an overly fast PowerPoint.

"You do?" James squawked.

Rachel grinned. "Yes." Shifting her weight, Rachel touched him softly on his forearm. "Where do you . . ."

An announcement over the loudspeaker abruptly cut Rachel off. Rachel quickly pulled her hand away. They all turned toward the stage and looked.

"Good morning, everyone." Patrick, the former student body president, tapped the microphone to make sure it was on. He continued after the room became quiet. "Please listen up. We're leaving for the hike. A nice picnic lunch will be set up for everyone to enjoy at the top." He continued to give instructions about the hike.

James didn't hear the rest, because his mind was fixated on Rachel, who stood only inches from him. Her hair radiated a sweet aroma, making his mind fuzzy. Though they weren't touching, his body ached to move a smidge closer, to cross the space holding them apart. To allow his arm to brush against hers. *Whoa, stop. Don't scare her off. Stay in the moment.*

Patrick droned on. "Okay folks, let's head out the back doors. I'll lead the way." He motioned with a big wave.

Immediately, the room buzzed. Many stood, pushing in their chairs. People moved their way toward the back double doors. In the middle of the hustle and bustle, Rachel and Haley grabbed some fruit from the table beside them before blending into the crowd. He lost sight of them in the shuffled. His heart sank. James had no other tricks up his sleeve. The five-dollar bill was the only thing he had been sitting on. How could he possibly find another way to talk to her without pressing his luck?

Several feet in front of him, some of his former classmates erupted into laughter. Dead center of the boisterous group was none other than Brandon. His stomach clenched, and his jaw locked. *Let it go. Avoid. Avoid. Avoid. Don't let him get to you.*

James slowed his speed to widen the gap between himself and Brandon. He certainly didn't want to spend the entire hike clipping at that guy's heels. Lost in thought, a hand gripped his shoulder. He turned his head, tracing the hand to the person's face. Ryan had found him in the sea of people. Chloe was firmly attached to his side, looking extra comfy beside him.

Ryan released his grip on his shoulder. "James, I found you," said Ryan, slightly out of breath.

James couldn't help but smirk. "You did . . ." His voice trailed off as he glanced over at Chloe. Then he leaned in and whispered to Ryan, "Though I can see I wasn't missed."

All shuffled forward toward the exit. A moment of understanding passed between the two friends. Nothing more was said. Eventually, they made their way through the double doors to the outside. The morning heat greeted him as the familiar Cloverton smells of lemongrass and dew danced at his nose. A steady stream of his former classmates made their way to the sidewalk, leading them across the hotel grounds to a wide and spacious dirt trail. They entered the trail with large trees lining both sides. With the trees providing needed shade, it made the temperature comfortable enough for hiking, even in the early summer.

After walking for a few minutes, James attempted to start a conversation. "Chloe. Tell me what you've been up to over the last ten years."

They took up half the width of the path. But even with three people across, it still allowed people coming down the hill to pass them.

Chloe laughed nervously, fiddling with some loose strands of hair. "What do you want to know about me?" She tilted her head forward past Ryan to meet James's glance.

"Start at the beginning, high school graduation." James turned his attention to the dirt path, making sure he didn't stumble over the upcoming rocks. "You graduated. You're young and adventurous, and the world is your oyster." James made a wide sweeping motion with his arm. "What did you do next? Go."

Chloe lit up. Quickly, she told them all about attending college, and her career as a teacher. Luckily, she chatted enough to keep his mind off Rachel. Knowing Rachel was somewhere in the sea of people was eating him alive, and he resisted the urge to run ahead and search for her.

Ryan kept the conversation going, asking the needed questions. James jumped in every now and then with a comment or two. After about an hour, they reached the summit, giving way to a nice grassy area. It overlooked Cloverton and the surrounding valley. Up there, the view was breathtaking.

With labored breathing, James took in the luscious landscape as it eased onto the flatter land. He had forgotten how beautiful their tiny town was in the summer. For a split second, he wondered how different his life would have been if he had stayed instead of fled. Immediately, a wave of repressed memories consumed him. His nostalgia was fleeting. He remembered he had made the right choice for himself. To leave.

The grassy area filled up as people trickled up from the trail. As Patrick had promised, the reunion committee had miraculously set up a picnic for all. There must have been a way to drive up, but he hadn't seen it. Nevertheless, he was grateful.

Seconds ticked by, and his breathing evened out enough for him to speak. "We made it!" James declared.

Ryan added, "At least the way back is all downhill."

Chloe chuckled like Ryan was the funniest guy on earth. She playfully touched his forearm with one hand while fluffing her hair with the other. "Please, don't tell me that was a struggle for you?" She raised an eyebrow. "It was practically flat the entire way. At least until that last little part at the end."

Ryan shook his finger. "Easy for you to say, miss aerobics instructor."

"Oh stop," replied Chloe. She hit him again, but this time on his bicep. "I told you I only teach one class on Saturdays at the local rec center."

"Well, it shows." Smirking, Ryan's glance ran down Chloe's lean, toned frame. "You look fantastic."

James rolled his eyes at their lame attempts at flirting. He stopped listening and scanned the crowd for Rachel. With a little planning, he might find a way to eat lunch with her. His heart skidded to a halt when he found her in the crowd, like the light had suddenly changed from green to red.

Rachel wasn't alone. Brandon had his arm around her shoulders. Boom. It was like a sucker punch to the gut. The guy *always* won. Was Brandon's path always paved in gold? He could have any woman. Any woman! Why Rachel? His shoulders drooped as he was forced to listen to Ryan and Chloe continue to exchange their flirty banter. His own personal circle of Dante's Inferno.

CHAPTER FOUR

"New York City," Brandon stated.

Brandon used his free hand to run it through his messy, dark hair. A move he no doubt probably practiced in front of the mirror. And boy did it work. Worked way better than she cared to admit.

"The big city," Brandon continued.

With Brandon's free arm sprawled casually across her shoulders, her gut raged with fire. Body ignited, Rachel found it hard to concentrate on anything other than his arm around her.

Brandon had joined their little hiking group when they reached the summit. Without any sort of reservation, he had placed his arm around her shoulders when he approached them. Everyone knew Brandon was a shameless flirt. Putting his arm around her meant nothing to him. Deep down she knew this, because she had watched him do it to practically every single woman at the reunion. But still, she was swooning harder than her sixteen-year-old self anticipating her first kiss.

Brandon, *the Brandon*, singled her out. Okay, maybe not singled her out, but he at least now acknowledged she existed.

Grinning like a total fool, Rachel snapped back to the conversation. "Yes, New York City." She managed to playfully nudge him with her elbow. "I know you don't venture out of Cloverton much, but have you ever heard of it?" *Cringe. Cringe. Stop it. Back it up, you little eager beaver. You sound ridiculous.*

Brandon paused. The air between them was practically pulsating with the steady beat of her heart. His jaw locked. "I might have." He shrugged. His eyes took on a dark, moody flicker.

He had no idea how bad she had it for him. Or worse, maybe he did?

Rachel leaned a tad too much into his arm. "I'm glad to hear you've left Cloverton at least once in the past *ten* years." It came out harsher than she wanted. Her weak attempt at flirting came across as an insult. Immediately, she regretted her words. "I didn't—" she stammered.

Brandon slid his arm off her shoulders. His neck and shoulders tensed, making the veins down his neck pop. She wanted to scream that she was only joking. It wasn't meant as a jab at his choice to remain in Cloverton. Hey, her own brother still lived here, and he was happy. But she knew enough to know that Brandon had little patience for anything other than total adoration.

"Ah, I've been lots of places." Brandon's eyes narrowed.

The coldness with which he stared back at her sent a shiver down her spine.

Brandon continued, "I don't know what you were trying to imply." He brushed off a little dust on the edge of his t-shirt.

Her heartbeat rang in her ears as heat seared its way across her cheeks. "Sorry . . ." Rachel stumbled over her words. Sweat gathered on her brow, and she swiped it away. "I didn't mean anything by it. Cloverton is a great place to live. I—I—"

Brandon straightened his shoulders. "It is a great place to live. Not that I really care about your opinion." He stepped further away from her. "Excuse me, *Rachel*, Haley. Enjoy your lunch." His tone was brash.

Then he pivoted and left.

Snap, and her tiny sliver of hope vanished in an instant. Her stomach plummeted. Rachel tracked his movements, watching as he moved to another batch of overly eager women, at the ready to listen to his every word. She had been swept away in the moment, thinking it meant something. Thinking he could enjoy the real her. He hadn't. Brandon only wanted a woman who bent to his every whim and constantly boosted his ego. She wasn't equipped to offer that. Somehow, she had imagined a picture of him which was a far cry from reality. Maybe the passing years had fabricated Brandon into a man who simply didn't exist? Or maybe she had grown up enough to know her desires had changed?

Sighing, Rachel glanced back at her hiking group. Plastering a smile on her face, she attempted to hide her shaky hands by forming them into tight fists at her side. "Should we get in line for lunch?"

The group agreed, walking over to the food line. Dragging her feet, Rachel hung back hoping for a moment to discuss the interaction with Haley.

Haley looped an arm around her elbow and whispered, "Don't worry about Brandon. You didn't do anything wrong. Certainly not anything that should've caused that sort of reaction."

They approached the food table, separated from those they had hiked with, but Rachel was relieved to be alone with Haley. She grabbed a plate along with utensils.

Lowering her voice, Rachel leaned closer and said, "It was weird, right?" Loading her plate with a sandwich and salad.

Haley moved along the table. "Yeah, he totally overreacted. You weren't trying to insult him." She elbowed her. "I mean, your flirting could use a little work. But that's not your fault."

Rachel rolled her eyes as she selected a sandwich and chips. "Ha. Ha. Hilarious."

A voice from the other side of the food table interrupted their conversation. "Looks like you two survived the hike." James grinned with his warm, bright, welcoming demeanor, a stark contrast to Brandon. "I didn't think the last part at the end would ever be over."

Startled, Rachel nearly dropped her plate. Shifting her weight, she tightened her grip around her food. Behind James in line was Ryan and a woman who looked vaguely familiar. They, too, stopped talking and stared at her.

Gnawing on her bottom lip, she replied, "Yes." Rachel managed a smile. "We survived . . . barely."

"Ryan too," piped up the woman next to Ryan.

Then both went back to loading their plates with food. James continued down to his side of the table opposite her. His brow glistened with sweat. Earlier, she hadn't noticed how his shirt stretched across his broad shoulders. She did now—that and more. A lot more. Like his obviously trim abs. Like his perfectly chiseled jawline. Like. Like. Like . . . Her throat became dry, and she failed to form a sentence of more than a few words.

"If I remember correctly, you were quite the runner in high school." James casually placed some salad on his plate. Then he grabbed a bag of chips. They both shuffled along the table. He continued, "Maybe hiking is different?"

Rachel arrived at the end of the table. Bending down, she pulled a soda out of the big tub of drinks. "I think it is. Haley might disagree with me." She stood again, balancing the cold soda and her plate of food. "She's one of those weird people who loves to hike." She tilted her head toward Haley.

"Hey, I'm not weird." Haley reached down and took a water bottle out of the ice bucket, shaking off the condensation. She nudged Rachel. "This one will run a marathon for *fun*." She rolled her eyes, then scanned the picnic area for a place to sit.

James lingered at the end of the food table. "Now that's just plain wrong." He smiled broadly, making her middle pool with warmth.

Nodding, Haley threw her free hand up. "Finally, someone who agrees with me."

Rachel scoffed. "A real tag team, you two." Then she laughed, feeling more at ease since Brandon had abruptly left her.

Cheerfully, James asked, "Is it okay if I sit with you two for lunch?"

Ryan joined them with his lady friend in tow. "Where are we sitting?" He took in the group.

Haley spoke up. "Why don't we find a table with enough space for all of us?"

She didn't wait for a reply, but started toward an empty table. All followed her across the grassy area to where there were still several empty picnic tables.

Over her shoulder, Rachel asked the woman next to Ryan, "Could you remind me of your name?"

"Chloe." Chloe slid onto the picnic table bench, placing down her drink and plate of food. "I remember both of you fondly."

The rest settled down at the table, too. Haley and Rachel sat across from Ryan, James, and Chloe.

Twisting off the cap of her water bottle, Chloe took a swig. Setting the bottle back down, she continued, "I ran cross country with you, Rachel."

A flash of recognition entered her mind. "Oh, you're right." She snapped, then pointed. "I'm sorry I didn't remember right away. I recognized you, but couldn't remember how our paths had crossed." Rachel opened her bag of chips, popping one into her mouth. "I obviously have a horrible memory."

Chloe waved it off. "No problem. I didn't run our senior year, *plus* we all look so different." She glanced down at her plate, then speared a piece of her salad and took a bite.

A beat of silence.

"Not everyone," piped up James.

All turned and glanced at him. He squirmed in his seat. His cheeks reddening.

Clearing his throat, James continued, "All I'm saying is not *everyone* looks different." He locked eyes with Rachel from directly across the table, like he and she were having a private conversation. "Some of us look exactly like how we looked in high school." Smirking, he bit into his sandwich without breaking eye contact.

Fire raged in her gut, and finally Rachel glanced down at her plate. Her palms sweaty, she wiped them on her black leggings.

"There are a few lucky ones who haven't seemed to have aged one bit," Haley agreed. "Like Rachel." Haley bumped shoulders with Rachel.

Ryan laughed. "Personally, I'm glad I look nothing like how I looked in high school." He leaned in closer to Chloe. "I've managed to only get better looking." He wiggled his brows.

James rolled his eyes and scoffed good-naturedly. "Don't worry ladies, he can sign autographs after lunch."

"What can I say?" Ryan inflated his chest, then theatrically spread his arms open wide. "Time has been good to me."

Chloe rested her elbow on the table, cradling her chin. Her gaze squarely on Ryan, she murmured, "It certainly has . . ."

Rachel and Haley exchanged a look. The rest of the lunch passed pleasantly. Rachel refused to look in the direction of Brandon, whose self-important laughter rang multiple times. Chloe and Ryan inched closer and closer to one another. And James's gaze never left Rachel. Haley kept constantly nudging her with her foot under the table.

When lunch ended, Patrick made an announcement that it was time to hike back to the hotel. Rachel and Haley slid out of the picnic bench, gathering up their trash. Throngs of people all moved at once, and Rachel lost sight of James and his friends once more. Rachel and Haley walked to the start of the trail in silence. Her thoughts were scattered. She had managed to scare off Brandon. He simply wasn't interested.

James seemed great, but she worried she'd mess that all up, too.

Rachel glanced down at the dirt trail. "Being back here, seeing everyone . . . it makes me acutely aware of the fact that I am solidly single. And clearly behind." Her stomach twisted itself from the revelation. "How am I ever going to find a guy? Brandon clearly didn't like what he saw."

"You're not behind." Haley moved to the side so a faster group, biting at their heels, could pass them. Once the group passed by, they continued walking. "You're twenty-eight years old! I just happened to find love young. And you're the total package. Any guy would be lucky to date you."

"Thanks," Rachel muttered, though she didn't believe her for a minute. If any guy would be lucky to have her, why wasn't she with any of them?

Her bun had loosened. Rachel stopped on the trail. "Give me a second." Ripping the rubber band out of her hair, she tossed her head forward to gather up the loose strands.

Haley waved. "No problem." She leaned forward, placing her hands on her knees. "It gives me a moment to catch my breath."

Once Rachel firmly secured all the strands in her hands, she flipped her head back.

Suddenly from behind her, James said, "Whoa . . ."

With her hair still gathered in her hands and rubber band between her teeth, Rachel quickly pivoted to face him. Her eyes dilated.

With a twitching smile, James said, "If you wanted me to help you with your hair, all you had to do was ask."

Her cheeks burned. Rachel finished securing her hair, then threw her hands down at her side. "Sorry." Gnawing on the inside of her cheek, she added, "I didn't see you there."

James wistfully sighed. "You never have." He plunged his

hands into the pockets of his athletic shorts. His cheeks tinged pink. Shaking his head, he averted his glance away from them. His chest heaved as he slowly exhaled. "Forget—forget I said that." He ran a hand through his hair.

Gulping, Rachel replied, "I can see you now." She boldly held his gaze, not wanting the moment to pass by without acknowledging it. "I want to see you." Each word she accentuated.

James kicked some of the dirt in front of him. "Maybe, but . . ." He waved a hand. "Forget I mentioned it."

James glanced down at the trail ahead. Rachel did the same, spotting Brandon several yards in front of them flirting with a bunch of women. Her stomach churned. She wondered what she had ever seen in Brandon. He wasn't at all like the fantasy she had created in her head.

James cleared his throat, snapping Rachel back to their conversation. "Brandon's up there." He made a head nod in the direction of Brandon. "Maybe you want to join him? You can catch him if you hurry."

Rachel paused, holding his gaze. "I don't want to catch up with Brandon."

James knew. He knew she had been hung up on Brandon. Did everyone know? The thought made her cringe at her obvious obsession with him. But something shifted within her. Maybe she had spent the last ten years pining for Brandon, but it didn't mean she needed to spend the next decade of her life doing it all over again. Brandon had fogged her mind and impaired her judgement. All those years of wanting—wishing—were hard to throw away in a single day. But here James admitted he was interested in her.

James rubbed his jaw. "I have a hard time believing that."

"I—um—" Rachel stumbled over her words. Her mind was a jumbled mess of memories and emotions. "I don't know." She failed to form the words she needed to say.

When she failed to continue, James held up a hand. "It's fine. I get it." He picked up his pace. "Excuse me." A few feet in front of them, he peered over his shoulder. "I'm going to go catch up with Ryan and Chloe."

James strode rapidly through the various groups until he was out of her view.

Once gone, Rachel jutted her chin at Haley. "What?" Her voice was overly accusatory.

Haley raised an eyebrow with a half smirk. "I didn't say anything."

"You didn't have to." Rachel smoothed out her hair, though she had only just pulled it up. "It's written all over your face."

Haley nodded, but she remained quiet. The path evened out, and the view of the hotel creeped into their line of vision.

"Okay." The silence eating Rachel alive. She threw her arms up. "James is hot. There I said it. But even more, I'm mortified he knew I have a thing for Brandon."

"Who cares about Brandon?" Haley waved the whole thing off. "Clearly, James likes you. Focus on that. I wouldn't let a good thing pass you by."

The words washed over Rachel, settling into the pit of her stomach. Maybe Haley was right. And maybe she should listen. But the thought of being vulnerable made her hesitate. What if she did explore things with James, only to find out he didn't like the real her either?

Rachel shrugged. "Let's see how the rest of the day goes."

Haley nodded. Their steps met the smooth concrete sidewalk, spilling back onto the hotel grounds.

Let's see. The words rang back and forth in her mind, over and over in an endless loop all the way back into the hotel.

CHAPTER FIVE

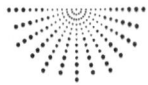

With shaky hands and a cold sweat slathered across his forehead, James half walked and half jogged the rest of the trail. Passing by other classmates, he attempted to find Ryan and Chloe, but failed to locate them. Recoiling at his latest attempt to talk to Rachel, James knew it was time to stop trying. He had never been smooth with women. He knew that. In his work as an attorney, James took on a different persona. A persona where he was confident, well-spoken, and respected, but clearly this didn't transfer to his personal life. James crashed and burned. Every. Single. Time. This time topped all his past failures by one thousand percent.

With the hotel in view, a hand gripped his shoulder. "James, do you want to come play pickleball with us? We need a fourth."

James glanced up to see Todd, who had been in a few of his classes and was with two of his former classmates. They had reacquainted themselves last night at Wilson's.

James shook his head. "Thanks for the offer, but I have some other plans. I'll see all of you tonight."

"Bummer." Todd released his grip. "Suit yourself. See you tonight."

Todd and his friends walked toward the tennis courts-turned-pickleball courts. James pivoted in the opposite direction, straight past the hotel. Eventually, he spilled onto Main Street. With a budding romance beginning between Ryan and Chloe, he knew he wouldn't be missed. Ryan deserved love as much as the next guy, and being a true friend, James figured he would do the potential love match a favor by getting lost for a few hours.

Wandering past the shops of Main Street, a wave of memories washed over him. Memories he had safely tucked away for years. But being here, in Cloverton, there was nowhere to hide. His mom had died when he was a child, and James hadn't thought about her in forever. It wasn't that he hadn't loved his mom, in fact it was the opposite. But when he remembered all he'd lost, he became debilitated. Like he couldn't breathe. Like the ache in his chest would refuse to leave. Like the world around him would never stop spinning off its axis. Like the pain was all consuming, swallowing him up, and refusing to let him go.

They say time heals all wounds, but James begged to disagree. If anything, he had only learned how to avoid triggering places, rather than repair his scars. His mom was the last person who had loved him. Those few short years he remembered with her in them were the only ones in his entire life where he knew that he was loved. Years had passed, and James was still all on his own. Sometimes the weight of loneliness bore down on him, and he had no choice but to push through it.

He stopped in front of the local toy shop. Peering through the front window, James smiled. A memory from when he was six popped back into his head. His mom had taken him there to pick out whatever he wanted for his birthday. It was one of his best and most vivid memories with her. Soon after, she had become sick, spending years in and out of the hospital. The last years of her life, she had been too sick to do anything more than sleep. But that day, it had been a good day before all the bad ones that followed.

If he closed his eyes, he could almost remember the feeling of his hand in hers. He could almost remember her signature scent of cinnamon and oranges. It was ages ago. A whole different lifetime. So much had changed since then, including himself.

His childhood had not been a happy one. His mom's sickness and eventual death made his dad, Timothy, a bitter and resentful man. James had been a victim of Timothy's sharp tongue and anger. James became the target of all his father's pain. In a particularly nasty moment, Timothy had revealed that he had never wanted a child, but had only agreed to appease his wife.

Within months of his mom's passing, Timothy remarried a woman who had zero interest in James. James's very existence annoyed her. He was a person she was forced to put up with, to be with Timothy. Instead of love, James received coldness and irritation. Though Timothy claimed he hadn't ever wanted James, Timothy quickly had two children with his new wife. Those were the children Timothy loved. Not him. James was a reminder of all Timothy had lost.

To survive, James kept quiet. He learned the art of being invisible, of not taking up space, or being in the way. The minute James graduated from high school, he packed his bags and took the little money he had managed to save from his job delivering pizzas, and he left. And he didn't look back or return, for anything, not even Thanksgiving or Christmas. Nobody missed him or checked in. Timothy never called. Not once. Once James no longer had contact with Timothy, he tried to erase the years of pain he had endured without his mom. This meant never visiting Cloverton. It meant forgetting about the town and the people.

For the most part, it worked.

Then out of the blue, his stepmom called. To this day, James doesn't know how she found his number, but in between sobs she revealed Timothy had died suddenly of a heart attack. James had simply replied, "Okay." The man she was crying about wasn't his father. James didn't have one. Instead of hanging up, James managed to listen long enough to get the details for the funeral.

As a surprise even to himself, he ventured back for the first time to Cloverton for his dad's funeral. Maybe he had longed for peace. Maybe he had wanted to forgive. But as he slipped into the chapel as the service began, his stepmom and her kids weeping in the front pew, James realized returning had been a mistake. Instead of closure and peace, his heart was filled with anger and rage. The preacher went on and on about what a great guy Timothy had been, a real family man. James found it hard to breathe. He gripped the pew in front of him so hard, his knuckles had turned white. A real family man, please. Did *real* family men cast out their child to make room for new ones?

Before the service ended, James left without even giving his stepmom his condolences. To this day, she probably never knew he had shown up. But as he peeled out of the church parking lot, James vowed then and there never to return to Cloverton. Just being in Cloverton made his throat itchy and skin crawl. Yet here he was, again, breaking his promise, all because of some childish, unrealistic hope he still held that Rachel might choose him.

The retail section of Main Street ended, giving way to widely spaced houses.

Lost in thought, James continued walking past the beautifully manicured lawns, long driveways, thick trees, and large homes. Without realizing it, his feet carried him all the way home. Startled, he nearly tripped on the curb leading to the curved driveway. He halted, staring up at the single story, ranch-style house of his childhood. Through the grapevine, James learned that his stepmom had moved away shortly after his father had passed. He didn't fear running into her, which was a relief. The home had been repainted and new wood siding and shutters had been added. If it wasn't for the same sturdy oak tree standing in the far corner of the front yard, he might have believed he was on the wrong street. But the rows of rosebushes wrapping around the house to the backyard were a dead giveaway. A tsunami of emotions hit him. Ones he wasn't equipped to process.

Stumbling backward, James almost fell as he moved away from the house. Nausea overtook him as acid burned his throat. Gripping his chest, James pivoted, bolting in the opposite direction. Fast. He needed to get away. To be anywhere but *there.* His childhood home was opening a Pandora's box of miserable years. Years he never wanted to remember. Years tainted with the feeling of being unwanted and unloved.

Making a quick right onto another street, James picked up his pace, morphing from a manageable run into a full dead sprint. His lungs burned, gasping for air. He pushed himself as hard as possible. The street up ahead dead-ended into a grassy park with a playground. The playground he often rode his bike to as a child.

It was only when his feet hit the crisp, crunchy grass that he managed to stop. Leaning forward, James gasped for air while he rested his hands on his knees. Slowly, breath by breath, his labored breathing returned to normal. His mind pushed back at the painful memories, tucking them carefully back into the box and locking them inside.

Why had he come back when he had vowed never to return? That mystical pipe dream with Rachel, of course, had challenged his vow. Then he remembered Rachel from back then. Smiling for the first time, James took in the view of the park with the playground structure at the other end. This had been the park where he had fallen in love with Rachel.

The day he fell in love with her had been just a day. A normal one. A day which blew through like all the ones before, and all the ones which came after it. But for him, it had been more than a day. It had been *the* day.

On that day, he was eleven years old as he swung back and forth on the swing, crying. His mom had passed away the year before. The loneliness he experienced following her death ate him alive, forcing him further and further into his protective shell. Swinging ever so lightly, he dragged his feet, making a hollow in the wood chips. Dust swirled all around, and then Rachel caught his eye.

He hadn't seen her before, and he was mesmerized by her. No longer a young child but not yet a teenager, stuck between the awkward forgotten space of time, he was shot with Cupid's arrow. Rachel ran all through the playground, laughing while her blonde hair fluttered behind her. The sun high in the sky cast a brilliant light over her, making her gleam. For a half hour, he watched from the swing as she played with her friends. The lightness in her laugh tugged at his broken heart.

Next thing he knew, Rachel ran over to the swings, taking the one next to him. With a Snickers bar in her hand, she peeled back the wrapper. Before she took a bite, she glanced at him, and their eyes locked. She stopped, bringing the Snickers bar down from her mouth. He tried to muster a smile, but he couldn't manage one.

In one swift movement, Rachel broke off half her Snickers and held it out to him. "I think you need this more than me," she said.

He muttered something. His heart in his throat made it hard for him to speak. He tried again. "You don't have to share."

A wide smile spread across her face. She shook the Snickers bar at him. "But I want to share. Take it. It'll make you happy."

If only it was that easy.

"Thanks," James replied. The corners of his mouth curled up in a shy smile. He accepted half of the Snickers bar and took a bite.

"See? You're feeling better already." Rachel beamed.

Smiling, Rachel flipped her hair over her shoulders, making the shiny strands glisten in the sunlight. At that moment, James marveled at her beauty and kindness, all wrapped up into one.

For a while, they both ate their Snickers in silence. He dragged his feet to keep from swinging too high.

Once done, Rachel stood, wiping her hands on her jeans. "I'll see you around."

Speechless, James gazed up at her. He managed a simple nod.

Rachel ran back off to play with her friends.

And that had been it. James was in love, and he went on loving her, and never managed to stop.

Over the years, James remained invisible to Rachel. In high school, the two of them had a few classes together. James lived for the days when he could pass her a pen, answer a question about an assignment, or work with her on a group project. The thing about loving someone for that long, you forget there ever being a time when you didn't love them. Back then, he was timid and shy, too afraid to put his feelings out there. He was constantly rejected at home, and a rejection from Rachel would have completely broken him. But now James had changed, grown. Maybe it was wishful thinking to believe Rachel could appreciate the newer version of himself.

James glanced at his watch. A few hours had passed since the hike while James pondered over his memories of Rachel, intertwined with the highs and lows of his childhood. Only a couple of hours remained until the main dinner event. Wandering back through the park toward the row of houses, he took the long path back to the hotel. Consciously, he avoided his childhood home.

James made it back to his hotel room, pushing open the door. "Ryan, are you in there?" He hesitated before he continued all the way into the room.

"I'm here!" Ryan shouted. "Come on in."

James crossed the threshold, wandering down the short hallway that opened up to the room with two queen beds.

Sprawled on his bed, Ryan had showered and was watching a basketball game on the TV

Ryan glanced up at his roommate's arrival, muting the TV. "Where did you wander off to?" He raised an eyebrow. "I was beginning to worry about you."

Pulling off his running shoes, James tossed them next to his bed. "I figured I'd give you and Chloe a little space to do your thing." He smirked.

The heaviness of seeing his childhood home evaporated into thin air as he shoved his past tightly back where it belonged.

"I appreciate that, but you don't have to stay away all week-end." Ryan made a hand gesture toward him. "I came here to spend time with you too. I don't want it to be weird between us."

James shuffled through the contents of his suitcase, gathering up his slacks and the blue button-down shirt he planned on wearing with a sports coat to the reunion dinner. "I know I didn't have to stay away." He peered over at him, smiling. "But I can see a love connection happening between you two, and I figured you needed a little alone time to explore things."

Ryan swung his legs over the side of the bed, sitting on the edge. "Chloe . . . man." He wiped a hand down his face, then slowly shook his head. "I really like her. Honestly, meeting someone this weekend had been the furthest thing from my mind. You know how I've been lately . . . since Chelsea."

Chelsea was Ryan's ex-girlfriend. The one he had dated for the last few years. Only three months ago, out of the blue, Chelsea ended their relationship. Since then, Ryan, a normally social and outgoing person, had not wanted to socialize at all. James and Ryan had commiserated enough evenings for Ryan to reveal how broken the entire relationship had left him. Chloe seemed to be bringing Ryan back to life, and James was grateful.

James shifted the clothes in his hands. "But it's a pleasant surprise. Right?" His voice trailed off.

"The best," Ryan chuckled.

"Anything to report?" James furrowed his brow.

Ryan paused, glancing over at him. "If you are asking in your non-subtle way if we've kissed, then the answer is . . . yes."

"I knew it." James scratched his chin. "Now, aren't you glad I managed to get lost for a little bit? You two only needed some alone time to make things happen."

With a wide arm gesture, Ryan said, "I made it happen, captain."

James rolled his eyes. "I think you've been watching a little too much of *The Office*."

"You know I love that show." Ryan did a fast chin lift. "Speaking of making things happen, how are things developing with you and Rachel?"

With clothes in hand, he froze. Him and Rachel. *If only*. Most likely, he had scared her away by overemphasizing his feelings for her. He had been making headway at lunch, but then he said too much when he saw her on the hiking trail. James wished he was better at flirting, dating, relationships, you name it. All the above.

His stomach churned and shoulders tightened. "I think I might've scared her off."

Ryan scoffed. "Doubt that. I saw her check you out a few times. She's at least attracted to you." Shaking his head, Ryan glanced back at the muted TV. "Plus, women loved to be pursued. It's in all those movies . . . what do they call them . . ." He waved the remote in his hand in a circle. "*Rom-coms*, the women live for that kind of thing. They act like they don't like you being too forward, but they secretly like someone showing they know what they want. Don't give up, because honestly, she would be lucky to get you."

"I don't know about that," James mumbled under his breath.

If she was lucky to get him, then why wasn't he *with* her?

"You're a good-looking guy. And you still have all your hair. A definite plus." Ryan stood, stretching. "And, somehow, you've managed to not get the dreaded 'dad bod'."

"What's a dad bod?" James asked, confused at some lingo he didn't know.

"Trust me, it's something you don't want." Ryan waved the whole thing off. "But no worries. You're good. Also, you're employed, always an extra point in your favor. And an attorney. Practically, all you have to do is not be a jerk, and you'll be golden."

"Umm . . ." James chuckled. "Okay." If only it really was that easy, but James wanted one woman. All the rest didn't matter if she wasn't interested. "Could you advertise that to the women here at the reunion? None of them seem to be buying what I'm selling." James took a few steps toward the shower, ready for the whole conversation to be over. "What time do we need to head down to dinner?"

Ryan unmuted the TV, settling back onto the bed. His eyes glued to the game, Ryan responded without looking over. "Six."

As he pulled his sports coat over his blue shirt, James gazed at his image in the mirror. All he saw was the little boy of the past staring back at him. Could one ever really escape their past? It seemed impossible. Like the chains of the past would forever be holding him back. Regardless, looking back at himself, James vowed this was his last night in Cloverton.

Forever.

He hated everything about this town. Tomorrow he was flying back to NYC, and he didn't plan on coming back. Not even for Rachel.

CHAPTER SIX

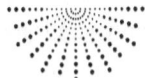

Blaring a notch too loud, the song *Time After Time* made Rachel's temples throb as she crossed the entrance into the banquet hall. A sizeable crowd was already gathered. Some were making their way through the dinner buffet, others were seated, and a few were dancing. Tables for ten fanned out around the dance floor, making use of every inch of available space.

Scanning the crowd, Rachel looked for Brandon. She hated herself for her secret obsession with having him in her peripheral vision. Tugging on the bottom of her inch-too-short, black cocktail dress, she made herself take a deep breath to calm her nerves. Then she spotted him, off in the corner talking with a group of people. Brandon was dressed in a navy suit with a blue checkered button-down shirt underneath. And he looked good—so good, it should've been criminal.

"I see Brandon," whispered Rachel into Haley's ear.

Loudly, Haley told Rachel to repeat herself. The song ended, and a moment of silence followed. Tracking Rachel's gaze, Haley crossed her arms. "Are we back to him already? I thought you didn't care about him anymore." Her voice didn't hide her annoyance.

With the music back on, Rachel spoke louder. "I know. I know, but for some reason I just want him to think I'm hot." She did a head tilt in his direction. "I have some weird obsession for him to realize he was an idiot, and then have him chase after me."

"You look fantastic. It's his loss." Haley's gaze flickered toward Brandon and then back to Rachel again. "I get it. He's your high school crush. Everyone has one, and they're hard to get over. But it's time to let it go. Isn't ten years long enough to be hung up on some idiot?" She popped an eyebrow.

Rachel chewed on the inside of her cheek. Brandon hadn't glanced her way at all. "You're right." She held her hands up in defeat. "I know you're right."

Haley looped elbows with her. "Let's get something to eat."

The two had already had a long discussion in the hotel room before coming down for dinner. It was time for Rachel to accept that the past was the past. Then a simple glimpse of Brandon made her throw all the progress she had made out the window.

"Fine." Her eyes narrowed. Brittany, former head cheerleader, was sidled up to Brandon. The two were laughing together. Her stomach clenched tight. Brandon wasn't worth taking up space in her mind. "Let's eat," Rachel replied.

The two wandered to the buffet line, loading their plates up with overcooked chicken and veggies. Scanning the room for an empty table, they settled into seats and started to eat. Rachel tried not to stare as Brandon reached out and brushed some hair out of Brittany's eyes. She wished they didn't look so good together, like both belonged out sailing on a yacht together.

"Stop staring. You're practically drooling." Haley nudged her with her elbow. "Enough." She shook her head and took a drink.

"What?" Rachel fiddled with her silverware, then forced herself to take a bite of the overcooked veggies on her plate. They tasted like cardboard, but she forced herself to swallow them. "Am I?"

"Yes," stated Haley. She twisted in her seat. "This would a be a perfect time for James to show up and take your mind off of Brandon." Unable to locate him, Haley turned back in her seat and cut into her chicken.

James. She wondered when he'd arrive. Rachel shrugged, turning her back to Brandon and Brittany so they were no longer directly in her eyeline. A few classmates filled in the empty seats at their table, and they ate and chatted for the rest of dinner. Her preoccupation with Brandon luckily dissipated.

As the meal wound down, Rachel turned to Haley. "I'm going to run to the bathroom. Did you want to come?" She pushed out her chair.

Haley shook her head. "I'm good. I see an old friend from the track team." She pointed in her friend's direction. "I'm going to go over and say hi for a minute while you're gone."

Rachel and Haley excused themselves from the table and went in their respective directions.

As Rachel entered the bathroom, she found it empty. Unzipping her clutch, she made a few touch-ups to her makeup. Once done, she entered one of the stalls and shut the door. A few seconds later, a group of ladies entered the bathroom laughing. The sound was a stark contrast to the solitude she had only moments prior. Her ears perked up as she tried to distinguish their voices from behind her closed stall door.

Then she heard, crystal clear: "You and Brandon make such a cute couple," said someone in an overly sing-song voice.

The group moved closer to the sinks and mirrors directly in front of Rachel's closed stall door. She eyed them through the small slit between the door hinge and wall. Her heart plummeted. Brittany, former head cheerleader, was standing in front of the mirror fluffing her hair.

"I know. By the end of tonight, he'll be mine, just like he should've been way back in high school, if Lyndsay hadn't stolen him from me." Brittany cleared her throat, fixing the outline of her lips with a single finger.

"So many women are after him tonight, but he's spent the whole night flirting with you," another unfamiliar voice added.

"You've got that right. And those other *pathetic* women are nothing I can't handle." Brittany threw her lipstick into her small purse. "Brandon and I had a good laugh over how aggressively some of these women are pursuing him. You remember Rachel, right?"

Rachel's blood ran cold. She prayed they didn't notice her hiding out in the stall.

"Yes," the voices eagerly said in unison.

"Brandon told me she can't take a hint. She's been practically trying to arm wrestle him the whole weekend. As *if* he would be interested in her."

The ladies all laughed.

Rachel's shoulder slumped. The confirmation of her worst fears came crashing down on her all at once. Inhaling, she pinched the bridge of her nose to keep from crying.

"Let's get out of here," said Brittany.

The door to the bathroom opened, then closed behind the group of ladies. Soon the bathroom became silent once more. When Rachel confirmed the coast was clear, she slowly opened the stall door, catching a glimpse of herself in the mirror. She stepped closer to the sink, washing her shaky hands. Slowly, she dried them off with a paper towel. *Don't cry. Don't cry. Don't. Cry.*

Glancing up, she blinked rapidly. Taking a few slow breaths, she willed herself not to get emotional. Who cared what a few bratty women thought? Right? Wrong. She cared. Too much. It was like she was fourteen years old all over again, awkward and unsure of herself, wanting nothing more than for the cool kids at school to ask her to sit next to them at lunch.

She stared at the image of herself in the mirror, taking in her dress, hair, makeup, her entire self. This weekend had been a mistake. Thinking she had some chance with Brandon was laughable. At the same time, she was glad she finally came to know the truth of his character on her own. It was something she had refused to listen to before, but now she had no doubt they weren't meant to be.

Come Monday, she would be back in NYC. Once back at work, this place and these people would become a distant fading memory. Cloverton was no place for her. Emotions finally in check, she fumbled with her clutch, opened it, and dug out her lipstick again. With the swift smooth strokes across her lips, her heartbeat steadied, returning to its normal pace one beat at a time. *You only need to survive tonight. Don't let those women get to you.*

Throwing her shoulders back, she tossed her lipstick back into her clutch and zipped it closed. It didn't matter what anyone said. Rachel knew she looked good, better than she had back in high school when she had a face full of acne and frizzy hair. Most importantly, Rachel was kind. She didn't sit around making fun of others. Nor would she sink to a level where she would retaliate.

Opening the door, she exited the bathroom, wandering back into the banquet hall. She scanned the room. Spotting Brandon, who was snuggled up close to Brittany, she sighed. Brittany could have him. She had crashed and burned. Brandon didn't care two bits about her, and it was time she stopped using up any of her energy thinking about him.

In the opposite corner, she spotted Haley surrounded by a bunch of her track friends. Rachel hadn't done track, only cross-country, and honestly, she had zero desire to go talk to people she had only known through Haley. Her shoulders dropped an inch.

With nothing else to do, she grabbed a drink, walking to the outside patio area connected to the banquet hall. She found it mostly empty, with only another couple sitting on the far side of the patio next to the firepit. The stillness of the night offered a welcome opportunity for her to regain her composure. In a minute, she would slap a smile on her face and go join Haley.

The patio overlooked the small downtown, which was lined with streetlamps, making it sparkle against the dark night sky. From up here, Cloverton looked small and quaint. Rachel moved over to the metal railing, taking in the view. A flood of memories came back from her high school years, some good, some bad, but she knew it was time to close this chapter of her life. NYC was home. Rachel was grateful for her job and friends she had in the city. She didn't miss living in Cloverton, even if it did look beautiful at night. A feeling of resolve overcame her.

Deep in thought, she hadn't noticed James join her on the patio.

"Want half?" James asked, holding up a chocolate chip cookie.

She flinched. Whipping her head, Rachel's gaze landed on James. His eyes sparkled back at her, reflecting the soft glow of the lamplight overhead. James looked *amazing*. She wondered how his perfectly grown stubble would feel under her fingertips. *Whoa. Where did that come from?* Heat splashed across her cheeks, and she forced her gaze back to the view of downtown.

"Say that again?" Rachel brushed some stray hairs out of her eyes, trying to not let his sudden appearance throw her completely for a loop. She shuffled her feet, stealing another glimpse of him.

His sports jacket stretched perfectly across his broad shoulders. Why hadn't she noticed him back in high school? His jawline was something dreams were made of. And those slacks with his tucked in shirt . . . *Yikes. Look up. Look. Up.*

"I asked"—James shook the cookie in his hand as he took a step closer to her—"would you like half?"

With his body intimately near her, she could smell his spicy aftershave mixed with hotel soap. His eyes were generous and kind, smoothing out the twisting feeling in the pit of her stomach. With a shrug and a half-smile, Rachel replied, "Sure, why not?" Her knees became wobbly.

He grinned, flashing her with his perfectly straight teeth.

Suddenly, ultra-aware of her appearance, she tugged her dress down. What did James see in her that she couldn't even see in herself? Surely, once he really knew her, he'd move right along to someone else. Like how it had happened before and would happen again.

Breaking the cookie in two, James held the bigger piece out to her. "Here."

"Thanks." Her hand grazed his as she took the cookie from him.

"No problem." James turned toward the railing and the view of Main Street.

For a minute, all she heard was the beating of her own heart. James took a bite of his cookie. She did the same.

Once he chewed and swallowed, James continued with his eyes glued forward, "It looked like you could use it."

Her temples throbbed. Breaking off another bite-size piece, she popped it into her mouth. She forced her attention from James out at the view, too. "What do you mean?"

Pivoting, James leaned his back against the metal railing, facing her. He took another bite of his cookie then casually replied, "I saw Brandon all over Brittany. Figured it might have —" James glanced past her toward the open double doors of the banquet hall. He cleared his throat, bringing his gaze back to her. "It might have been hard for you to see."

"I—" Rachel stumbled over her words. Shaking her head, she looked down at her feet. "I'm not worried about what Brandon is doing." Then she remembered to stand straight, and she pulled back her shoulders.

James popped the rest of his cookie into his mouth, wiping his hands on the napkin. Then he crumpled up his napkin, tossing it into the nearby trash can. It landed directly in the center of the bin.

James cleared his throat. "I know you had a thing for him back in high school, and I've—I've spent the entire weekend watching you, watching him." He took the two steps back to his place against the railing. Casually, he crossed his ankles and arms.

"I didn't realize . . ." Rachel darted her gaze away, biting down on her bottom lip. "I didn't think I was being that obvious."

Twisting she leaned her back against the railing too. Shoulder to shoulder, they faced the opened double doors leading to the party inside. Their bodies almost touched each other. His nearness made her heartbeat triple its speed. Rachel tried to focus, but his intoxicating scent made it a challenge.

Finally, because she had nothing to lose, Rachel added, "It doesn't matter. I'm over it. Brandon was a pipe dream, nothing more. A schoolgirl fantasy, but I can see now I've remembered him all wrong." She exhaled loudly, crossing her arms too. "He's a jerk."

She wondered why she never picked the good ones.

James laughed then nudged her shoulder. "Finally, something we can agree on."

Rachel tilted her face toward him, their eyes catching. His lips twitched at the edges. She stared, then James cleared his throat, making his Adam's apple bob back and forth.

"Sometimes I think it's exhilarating to chase after the dream— to go after the one you never thought you could have." James unbuttoned his sports jacket button and plunged his hands in his pockets. "I can understand . . ." He paused, then stammered. "Because—because that's what you are to me."

Stunned, Rachel didn't respond immediately. She was somebody's dream? James clearly was remembering her all wrong. Surely, his recollection of the past was cloudy.

"I . . ." Rachel stumbled over her words. "I don't know what to say."

Pulling one hand out of his pockets, James waved it off. "You don't need to say anything. But back in high school, and even before then, I was often overlooked and forgotten. It was a constant storyline in my life. But when I came this weekend . . . I only came for you. Only you could drag me back to this place and town that I hate more than anything." His jaw tightened as his gaze remained steady on the party inside.

Rachel shifted her weight. Her mind reeled. She didn't know what any of this meant. James remembered her. He had years of memories, where she had none. Maybe at some point she would remember him better, but maybe not. It made her unsettled that he had a head start.

Finally, Rachel chose not to acknowledge James's confession about her, but instead asked, "Why do you hate it here so much?"

James blinked, pausing. A loud commotion erupted inside the party, along with the sound of clapping. Neither moved nor tried to return.

He exhaled. "My childhood was less than ideal. Cloverton holds no good memories for me. You were the only bright spot. Everyone in my life I once had is now gone. There is nothing left for me here."

"I'm sorry to hear that." Rachel tilted her face toward him, letting her eyes glide over him. She studied him. "Sometimes . . . I guess it's best to leave the past behind. To start fresh."

"I've been trying my whole life to do just that." James leaned closer to her. "Some days I do better than others."

Before Rachel had a chance to respond, another round of applause rang from inside, carrying all the way outside. Rachel stood straight. "I wonder what's going on." She exchanged a look with him.

James smirked. "They're probably giving Brandon some kind of award."

Rachel laughed. The mood became lighter. "Highly likely. Probably the 'he's awesome, we're thrilled he showed up' award."

They both chuckled. Then it became quiet again.

Rachel took a step toward the open doors. "I think I should go find my friend Haley."

"Rachel . . ." James moved closer to her.

His gaze locked with hers. The intensity made her gulp. Her middle filled with warmth.

"I like you. I would love to take you out sometime." James reached into his pocket, pulling out a business card from his wallet. He held it out to her. "Call me if you're ever interested in meeting up."

Rachel reached out slowly, taking the business card from him. She glanced between the card and his face. "I . . . I . . . Thanks."

Before she had a chance to say anything more, James touched her lightly on the forearm. "Rachel, it was great seeing you again. You're just as lovely as I remember. I hope to hear from you." He pivoted in the direction of the open doors. Shifting, he added, "Bye."

James walked back into the party, leaving her lingering on the patio.

With sweaty palms, Rachel peered down at the business card. His office was only a few blocks from the hospital where she worked as a labor and delivery nurse. She walked by it every single day on her way home from work. What were the odds? Her heart rate picked up its pace. Though she had no intention of ever calling him. Slipping the card into her clutch, Rachel squared her shoulders and walked back into the party.

Back in the banquet hall, James willed himself to remain calm. His hands at his sides formed tight fists, capturing the nervous energy coursing through his veins. He was jittery, like he had downed a few espressos. And so not like a man who had somehow managed to place a full hand of cards in front of the woman he wanted more than anyone. *Rachel. Rachel. Rachel.* Maybe she would never call. Maybe this was the last time he would ever see her. Still, a smile slowly spread across his face, making him pull back his shoulders. He couldn't help but be proud of himself for taking a risk.

Scanning the extremely loud and overly crowded room, James eventually spotted Ryan in a secluded corner with his arm wrapped around Chloe. It looked like his friend would be leaving the reunion with a new girlfriend. James crossed the banquet hall toward them.

Startled, both glanced up at him when he approached. "Ryan, I'm calling it a night." He announced loudly over the pulsating noise.

Chloe released her death grip on Ryan's forearm as he stood.

"Please don't leave yet." Ryan raised an eyebrow and whispered, "I thought you were a man on a mission."

"I was—or rather, mission completed." James's chest puffed up a tad.

"You spoke to her?" Ryan smirked. "And?"

Slapping him on the back, James replied, "I did. And all I can say is, I can go back to New York and live with no regrets."

"I'm proud of you." Ryan nodded. "You finally went after what you wanted."

James glanced quickly at Chloe, who remained seated but appeared to be listening to their every word. "I'll see you back in the city. I have an early morning flight, so no need to wake me when you get back to our room. I'll be up and gone before you get up."

Mounds of casework were waiting for him back at his office. He needed to prepare for his Monday meetings. He waved at Chloe and said his goodbyes.

He left, silently bidding farewell to a room full of people who wouldn't remember him. James was happy to escape Cloverton and his Pandora's box of bad memories. At least now, he had one good memory with Rachel to counterbalance the bad.

CHAPTER SEVEN

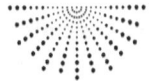

"Judy, do you have those documents I need for my ten o'clock meeting?" James approached his secretary, a woman in her late fifties with tightly curled brown hair.

Judy shuffled a few things on top of her desk. "I have the conference room all set up for you." She continued to search for the document. Locating it, Judy handed it to him. "Here you go."

"Thanks." James took the portfolio, flipping through the first few pages. "This looks great. I appreciate it." He glanced up. "The drinks and food are all set out?"

"Like I said." Judy pulled herself closer to her desk, wiggling her mouse around so her computer screen popped back on. "Everything is all set up."

"Sorry. I know you never drop the ball. I'm slightly nervous about this meeting." James almost added, *my entire career is hanging on it*. If he messed this up, then he'd be out on the street, but he held his tongue. Instead, he managed, "I appreciate all your hard work."

Judy smiled. "Anytime, boss." Her eyes were glued to her computer screen. "Good luck. I know this is a big account for you."

Though he had many important, high-profile clients, this was his biggest merger to date. Since he had returned from his high school reunion two weeks ago, he had lived and breathed this case. With practically zero down time, James didn't have time to dwell on the fact that Rachel hadn't called or texted him. Somehow, he had managed to crash and burn yet again. After playing the weekend's interactions on repeat in his mind for a few days, James finally decided he had done his best. If Rachel wasn't interested, and there was nothing he could do. Throwing himself into work became the perfect way to forget all about her.

Entering the boardroom, James took in the view of the nicely placed portfolios in front of each seat. A large spread of food and drinks were on the credenza against the wall. Taking a deep breath to calm his nerves, he walked toward the large wall of windows from the 69th floor high rise. New York City from this high up was breathtaking. Rachel was out there somewhere. *So much for not thinking about her.* But in a city of millions of people, Rachel might as well have been on the other side of the world.

In NYC, you rarely ran into people accidentally, not with its constant stream of individuals coming and going. Every day was filled with a different mass of folks getting on and off the subways. Those who walked by on the sidewalk strode at faster than normal paces. If one wanted to blend in, it was the perfect place. James loved being surrounded by others, even if they were strangers. The hustle and bustle of the city made his life feel less lonely.

Some shuffling outside the conference room broke his thoughts. With a smile plastered on his face, James pivoted and strode to the doorway to greet his clients, Mr. and Mrs. Masters, and fellow attorneys entered the conference room.

After the typical exchange of small pleasantries, all parties settled into their respective seats around the conference table. James started the meeting. "It's been a long road, but I'm happy to announce the other side has agreed to all our terms. They should be signing the agreement shortly." He pushed back the sleeve of his suit jacket, revealing his watch. "In about a half hour."

Mrs. Masters clasped her hands together. "Excellent news. The timing couldn't be better." She smiled over at Mr. Masters, then brought her attention back to James. "My husband and I are off on our month-long vacation to Italy."

"Wonderful. You two certainly deserve a break after the stresses of this merger." James flipped open the portfolio in front of him, motioning for them to do the same. "My associates and I will go over the terms of agreement with you before we conduct the closing call. We'll have you on your way to Italy in no time."

They'll be on their way, and he'll be here working around the clock to finalize every detail of their merger.

A pinch between his shoulder blades made James's neck ache. The stresses of the last two weeks started to take their toll. Brushing the discomfort aside, James launched into his long explanation of the merger. All eyes were on him, and his clients nodded at each major point he presented. Here in this board-room, James came alive as he displayed his competence and skills. The feeling invigorated his spirit, making him square his shoulders. His mind always became clear. Though his job was hard and demanding, it gave his life meaning and purpose. Being busy, he almost forgot about all the things he still wanted, like a wife and family.

If only Rachel, could see him here. If only she knew how much he could give her. *If only . . .*

CHAPTER EIGHT

"Okay Sarah, on the count of three you need to push." Rachel stood next to the expectant mother, checking the monitor for any signs of distress. At the end of the bed, the doctor was ready to assist once Sarah began to push.

Sarah, her patient, moaned loudly. Sarah's husband gripped her hand on the opposite side of the bed from Rachel.

"I can't do it!" Sarah wailed. Sweat glistened Sarah's brow, trickling down her temples. "I'm not ready to be a mother!"

Calmly, Rachel patted her other hand. "It's a little too late for that." Rachel locked eyes with Sarah. "You can do this."

Shaking her head, Sarah closed her eyes and breathed in and out.

Rachel continued, "You're going to be a wonderful mother. I just know it."

They were words Rachel had repeated numerous times to many expectant and new mothers. Words she knew could calm even the worst fears. Sarah wasn't the first, nor would she be the last who felt nervous about the unknown.

Appearing half delirious and half exhausted after nearly nine hours of active labor, Sarah moaned, twisting around in her bed.

Rachel knew she was trying to find a more comfortable position, something not possible during this point in the labor. Sarah tightened her grasp of her husband's hand while he spoke softly to her. The couple appeared to be in love. It warmed Rachel's heart. Only some who came into the hospital for the birth of a child had that type of love. Rachel hoped someday she'd find that love too.

Being a labor and delivery nurse for several years, Rachel had seen and heard everything. A gambit of births from teen pregnancy to later-in-life surprise pregnancies. Some deliveries were long and difficult, and others were quick and easy. Sometimes babies entered the world in the corridor, rather than a delivery room. Some expectant mothers might have to push for hours, while some might only give a single push.

With all their own unique challenges, every birth always left Rachel in awe. Women were amazing, willing to sacrifice from day one for their child. At the very first baby's cry, the room became filled with palpable happiness. In that single beautiful moment, Rachel reveled in the beauty of life and hope. Someday, with all her heart, Rachel hoped to experience the beauty of childbirth herself.

Dr. Grayson interrupted her thoughts. "You're crowning." He adjusted his rubber gloves, instructing Sarah to scoot as far as possible to the edge of the bed. "A few more pushes and your baby will be here. You can do it, mama."

"I can't do it." Sarah gripped the side rails of the bed. Closing her eyes for a moment, Sarah took long, deep breaths. "I'm too tired." Sweat trickled down her temples, soaking her hospital gown.

"Yes. You can." Moving to the head of the bed, Rachel supported her back and shoulders. "Now, push."

Giving one last push, Sarah wailed. A few seconds later, a cry broke the silence of the room. Sarah's husband kissed her on the cheek, then smoothed the top of her head.

Rachel smiled.

Dr. Grayson announced the couple had a beautiful and healthy daughter.

Weeping, Sarah reached out to take her newborn daughter from him.

Elated, her husband squeezed her shoulders. "You did it!" He exclaimed as tears misted his eyes.

Quickly, Dr. Grayson and Rachel worked in silent unison to help clean everything up. Rachel marveled at the instant love the couple had for their baby girl. Gingerly, Sarah traced the outline of her daughter's face while her husband slowly stroked her full head of hair. The tender exchange reminded her why she loved her job.

Once their job was completed, Dr. Grayson and Rachel slipped out into the hallway, allowing the new family of three some much-needed privacy.

In the hospital corridor, Dr. Grayson turned and said, "Another successful delivery," he grinned. "It's always a pleasure to work with you."

"Ditto." Rachel strode toward the nurses' station. "Now Dr. Grayson," she waved him off, "please go home to your family and get some sleep."

"You won't hear an argument from me." Dr. Grayson bid farewell.

Rachel arrived at the nurses' station to fill out the necessary paperwork. Her feet ached and stomach rumbled. A few moments later, Ellie, a fellow nurse and friend, threw her file folders down on the table next to her.

"We finally have a shift together." Smiling, Ellie flipped open the top file. "I was beginning to think you decided to stay in Cloverton forever."

"Nah." Rachel made a note on her file, picking up the next one from her stack. "It's big city living for me."

"How did your delivery go?" Ellie didn't pause long enough

for her to respond. "I'm ending my shift, but my current patient is hours away from delivery." With mischievous eyes, Ellie tilted her head. "Of course, I didn't let her know that."

Rachel smirked. "No good nurse would."

Both continued to fill out their respective paperwork, and right before Rachel finished, Ellie asked, "By the way, how did your reunion go?" She clicked her pen closed, shoving it into the top pocket of her scrubs. "Anything exciting transpire?" Folding her arms, Ellie leaned back against the nurses' station.

Her shoulders tightened, and Rachel stopped midway on her form. Where did she even begin? It had been over two weeks since her reunion, and she had failed to do anything with that business card James gave her. Partly because she was chicken, and partly because she had been picking up every extra possible shift to continue to save for her dream vacation to Barcelona. Only recently had Rachel managed to pay off her student loans. A goal only accomplished due to years of hard work and frugal living. Being single, she was determined to finally go somewhere fun, and something about Barcelona sounded simply dreamy.

James. James. James. So much time had passed since her reunion, Rachel had no doubt jinxed anything that may or may not have developed between them. If she called him, then she'd have to try—and trying meant putting herself out there. Brandon hadn't been interested in her, and she feared once James really got to know her, he might not like her either. Her fragile ego couldn't take the rejection.

Reaching across the tabletop, Rachel grabbed the stapler next to the computer. "High school reunion . . ." She shrugged while stapling the paperwork into the file. "It went fine. Nothing to report."

Ellie raised her eyebrow. "Huh. Did you or did you not see Mr. Teen Dream?"

Rachel cringed. "Brandon." She let out a long sigh, regretting wholeheartedly how desperately she had chased after him.

Ellie wagged a finger at Rachel. "Yes, Brandon." Her voice was overly high, swimming with innuendos. "I know you wanted a second chance with him."

"Ha, we never really even had a first go of it." Her jaw tightened. Rachel pinched the bridge of her nose. "I saw him. He's a jerk. End of story." She removed her hand and shook it off.

"Ahh . . . I'm sorry to hear it." Lightly, Ellie squeezed her arm. She lowered her voice. "You okay? I know you had a lot of hope riding on that weekend."

"Like I said, I'm fine." Her voice came out harsher than she wanted. Rachel gnawed on her bottom lip. "Sorry. It's been a long day." She tossed the file into the appropriate bin. "I did get another guy's number . . . but I haven't called him."

Ellie's eyes widened. "Details." She nudged her with a shoulder.

Quickly, Rachel rehashed the weekend with Ellie, ending with James giving her his business card.

"You need to call him." Ellie made a tsk sound with her tongue. "It's a slam dunk. Come on, Rachel."

Rachel's cheeks warmed. "I don't know. I'm so sick of dating. All the anticipation of a new possibility, only to have it crash and burn. I think I'm benching myself for a while."

Ellie countered, "A hot, fully employed guy gave you *his* number." She raised an eyebrow, giving her a pointed look. "You're not going to at least try and see if there's something there? I'd jump on that in a heartbeat."

When Ellie phrased it like that . . . maybe Rachel was being a little ridiculous.

"Besides," Ellie continued, "I'm sure it's way better odds than online dating."

"True. Online dating is the worst." Rachel couldn't help but laugh at her most recent dating disaster. "The last guy I met online claimed he was an entrepreneur and six-foot-four, but he ended up being shorter than me." She made a quotation sign with her fingers. "And quote entrepreneur meant he sold his stuff on eBay while living in his parents' basement. I couldn't get out of there fast enough."

Ellie chuckled, shoving her playfully. "See. That's the alternative. A complete desert waste land. Trust me, I know. Text *him*."

"He is cute . . ." Rachel's voice trailed off.

Rachel remembered how perfectly James's suit jacket tugged across his broad shoulders. And how her heart picked up its pace when he was near. The possibility of something new and great sounded amazing. What were the odds James was the one? Slim. *Whoa, calm down. Back that train up. It's a date. Nothing more. But at least give him a chance.*

"You've convinced me." Rachel smiled. "I'll text him."

Ellie tossed her files into the bin. "My job here is done in more ways than one. I'm off in five minutes. I'll see you soon." She backpedaled away from Rachel, pointing at her. "I want an update after you contact James. Promise?"

Rachel nodded. "Promise." She crossed her heart, gave Ellie a grin, and bade her goodbye.

Ellie might be done with her shift, but Rachel still had hours to go. She grabbed a granola bar from the basket of random snacks people had left, shoving it into her mouth. James would have to wait a little longer.

CHAPTER NINE

With his door propped open, James spotted Judy walking by. He paused his typing. His shoulders ached and neck screamed. The stress of the day seeping right into the night. Chained to his desk, James hadn't left his office all day. And now he was starving.

"Judy," James called out to her.

Judy stopped, ducking her head into his doorway. "Yes. Did you need something?" She stepped into his office.

"If you don't mind, I needed you to order me dinner." James shifted in his chair. "Unfortunately, it's going to be another late night for me."

"No problem. What would you like?" Judy asked.

"A burger and fries from that place around the corner." James grabbed his wallet and pulled out his credit card, holding it out to Judy. "Buy yourself something, too."

Judy took the credit card from him, fiddling with it in her hand. "Thanks. Did you need me to stay late tonight to help you with anything?"

James waved the idea off. "No. No. You can leave once the food arrives."

"Great," Judy grinned, then pivoted. "I'll order this right away and be back with it soon."

James turned his attention back to the document he was drafting, reevaluating the updates he had made to the agreement. Minutes ticked on by. Lost in deep concentration, the shaking of a brown paper bag jolted him.

James flinched, glancing at his doorway. Judy lingered.

"Back already." James stretched his hands high above his head.

With her purse slung over her shoulder, Judy gave him his order and left for the night.

Once again alone, James rose, walking to his wall of windows overlooking New York City. The city streets twinkled below him. Though he could only hear faint sounds from way up on his floor, he knew the streets were vibrant and alive. Yearning to be outside, if only for a few minutes while he ate, James grabbed his cell phone, sliding it into his pocket. With dinner in hand, he headed down the elevator, across the lobby, then outside to eat.

Being summer, the sun had only started to make its descent. The last little bit of sunlight seeped into his skin. James took a deep breath of the not-so-fresh air, heading to the square sandwiched between three other high-rise office buildings. It had a few shady trees and benches. Settling onto one of the benches, James pulled out his food box, popping it open. In solitude, he nibbled on a few fries while refusing to look at his email inbox for a full ten minutes. Instead, he forced himself to take a break from his constant worries. Eating alone was a common occurrence in his life. Some days he didn't mind, but tonight a loneliness enveloped him that he found hard to shake.

In a city with millions, you'd think it would be easy to find someone. It wasn't. Years had passed with no success. There had been a few relationships, but all fizzled out the same way. James blamed his long work hours, his lack of any family relationships, his skepticism of many women, along with a long list of other issues. Mindlessly, he flipped open his to-go box, trying not to think about his singledom. Then someone calling his name interrupted his thoughts.

The voice called again, louder. Twisting in his seat, James turned in the direction of the sound. Across the square, the shadowy figure of a woman approached. James set his to-go box on the bench next to him. He stood, taking a step toward the woman.

A second passed. The woman drew closer. Her image became clearer. Standing, James strained his eyes.

Was that really Rachel? No, it couldn't be. Was he dreaming?

Soon, the shadows on her face fell away, and she came into full view. He had no doubt. It was Rachel. Instantly his knees wobbled while the ground underneath him became unsteady. His stomach took a nosedive. This was happening. James remained stunned. *Come on brain. Work.*

"Rachel," James stated, pushing a hand through his messy, unkempt hair. His heart picked up to a steady staccato beat. "What—" He stammered, shoving his hands into his pockets. "What are you doing here?" He glanced around the square, looking past her to see if she was with someone he maybe hadn't seen. She was alone.

Breathless, Rachel stopped directly in front of him. "I thought that was you." She adjusted her purse strap, darting her gaze away for a moment before finding his eyes once more. "I couldn't believe it when I saw you across the square but here you are." She threw her arm down at her side.

Seeing her here, in *his* city, made the dream a surreal reality.

"Isn't this a coincidence . . ." James fiddled with the keys in his pocket. Catching himself, he forced himself to stop. He pulled his hand out, squared his shoulders, and met Rachel's eyes.

Rachel was dressed in scrubs and pink sneakers. She looked good. Real good. A perfect combination of casual and sexy—in scrubs, for crying out loud. His mind flashed to the dress she had worn the night of the reunion dinner. The dress of all dresses which hugged her body in all the right places. *Oh boy, hold it together. Focus.*

"I'm sorry I never called." Rachel wrung her hands together. Her cheeks tinted red, making his middle pool with warmth. "I wanted to . . ." Her voice trailed off. She gazed past him.

She wanted to call? Him?

James reached out, lightly touching her elbow. His fingertips instantly warmed. "No, really, it's fine. No explanation needed." There, he almost sounded normal, and not like he was on a treadmill sprinting at the highest speed. "I understand."

"I've been super busy with work." Rachel shuffled her feet, gnawing on her bottom lip. "Since the reunion, I have been working nonstop, and I get home late. And when I do, I practically crash face forward on my bed." She fiddled with the hem of her scrubs. "It wasn't that I didn't want to call—I did."

A huge group of boisterous people entered the square. Their talking and laughter vibrated back and forth, filling the space between them. Both peered in the direction of the noise, staring as they became louder and louder. James attempted to speak over the group, but it was fruitless.

Once the group exited the square, he turned his attention back to Rachel. "I understand. I've been extra busy and working around the clock too. Did you just get off work?" He nodded toward her outfit.

Rachel glanced down, smoothing out the top of her scrubs shirt. "Yes. I'm a nurse. I work at the hospital right around the corner. Honestly, I'm surprised we've never run into each other before—but then again, this is New York City." She gave a crooked smile.

A nurse? James couldn't help but smile back brightly. "What kind of nurse?"

Rachel's eyes lit up, and she straightened her back. "Labor and delivery," she said with pride.

"I'm impressed," James stated. This was his chance to be bold.

Before he had time to overthink things, he said, "You just got off work—you must be hungry. Do you want to go get something to eat with me?"

Rachel peered over his shoulder at the bench with the opened to-go box. "It looks like you already have dinner. Don't you?" She nervously laughed.

"Maybe," James shrugged. "But if you're free, then I don't." He grinned, catching the twinkle in her eye.

Her lips formed a slight smirk. "Okay." Rachel pushed some loose strands of hair behind her ears.

"Okay, you'll go have dinner with me?" James raised an eyebrow. "Or okay, you're an idiot please stay away from me?"

Rachel shifted her weight. "The former."

James threw his arms up. "Great, it's official, I'm an idiot."

Rachel's eyes dilated. Her cheeks darkened to crimson. "No . . ." She reached out and grabbed his forearm. "I meant," she spoke more slowly, "I'd like to go to dinner with you."

James grinned. "I thought you'd never ask." Then in one swoop he gathered his to-go box, tossing it into the trash. "Do you like Thai food?" he asked without skipping a beat.

"Love it." Rachel grinned, making her eyes sparkle.

All the impending deadlines, the stress, the overwhelming workload, the loneliness dissipated. Snap, and it was all gone. The world began to revolve around a sphere where it was only himself and Rachel.

Tugging down the hem of her underwhelming, oversized scrubs, Rachel tried to not feel overly self-conscious. But, in all honesty, she hadn't washed her hair in nearly a week. Most likely her messy, greasy updo screamed, *no longer trying*. With her work schedule, her self-care had taken a back seat.

In New York, the city where you *never* run into people you

know, she had run into James, sitting outside his office. Her stomach had done a weird somersault, while her mind quickly catalogued every romantic fantasy she didn't even know she had. Because, wow, James looked hot. Like it should be criminal to wear pants like that.

On the other hand, she looked like a damp dishrag. But here she was, in her ratty, oversized, not-even-new scrubs, about to have dinner with the man she had only decided hours ago to finally text. *Okay, God, I'm hearing you loud and clear. Don't worry, I will try my hardest not to mess this up.*

Rachel fell in step with James on the always overly crowded sidewalk. She didn't mind. It gave her an excuse to allow their arms to graze each other every now and then.

"It's only a few streets up." James gave her a sideways glance. "Are you okay to walk?"

So, he was thoughtful, too. Geez. How was he still single? Lucky for her, James was dressed up in business attire: dark blue slacks and a tightly checkered white and blue button-down. Him at the ready to impress, and her at the ready to lounge. This was so not how she imagined their first date going. There were probably layers of irony there that she would have to unpack later.

"I'm good." Though her feet had ached leaving the hospital, Rachel didn't feel the dull pain anymore. She tilted her head to the side, taking in his five o'clock shadow. "What's the place called?" She sidestepped a weird-looking pothole.

A huge stream of teenagers dressed in matching choir outfits spilled from the crosswalk onto the sidewalk beside them. The group was oblivious to other pedestrians. A few bumped into her without an apology, shoving her up against the wall of a coffee shop. James wrapped an arm around her waist, pulling her away from the inconsiderate choir group before they trampled her to death.

Startled, Rachel gripped onto his ripped bicep, regaining her footing. "Oh . . . thanks." The words tumbled from her mouth, settling in the small intimate space between them. Their eyes met, making her temples sound in her ears. James was close. Real close, and Rachel liked it. A lot. His spicy aftershave made her nostrils flare. "They don't seem to be aware that anyone else exists." The words came out all wobbly like the tremor in her knees.

The teenagers continued trailing by them, a long, endless stream of blue uniforms. Rachel didn't mind one bit, not with James's lingering hand on her waist. She felt warm and safe with him there. The group finally passed, making room for them to walk once more on the sidewalk.

"All clear." James released his hand, taking a step away from her. Then he rubbed the back of his neck. "Thai House." He cleared his throat. "That's the name of the restaurant."

Food? That's right, they were talking about food.

"I love that place," Rachel managed to say while fiddling with her purse strap.

They both continued down the sidewalk. Then, in unison, they both turned to one another and said, "I love their mango sticky rice."

Rachel laughed, making the nerves in her stomach disappear.

"It's the best." James grinned.

Rachel nodded. "I completely agree."

The light at the intersection turned red. They stopped, and James hit the crosswalk button. "I want to hear more about your job as a nurse."

"What about it?" Rachel said, allowing herself another glimpse of James.

His hair was slightly frizzy from the sticky, muggy air. She wondered what it would feel like to run her fingers through it, but she shook off the thought and made herself focus.

James tilted his head toward her. "Why labor and delivery? Why do you like it?"

The crosswalk light changed. James entered the intersection, and Rachel trailed along beside him. Once across the street, they made a right turn.

Rachel tried to remember what they were talking about. *Your job and why you picked it.*

"How long do you have?" Rachel teased.

"All night," James replied, not missing a beat.

Rachel knew she always became animated and excited when she talked about her job. She loved the exhilarating rush that came when a birth came fast and quick. Other days, with long and difficult births, she reveled in the beauty of pain. The mother making the ultimate sacrifice for their child. Every part of her job filled her soul and brought meaning into her life.

So, when Rachel started talking to James about all the things she loved about her job, she didn't stop until they arrived in front of the restaurant.

James held the door open for her.

Wringing her hands together, Rachel gnawed on the inside of her cheek while heat seared its way across her face and neck. "Sorry. I didn't realize I had been talking so much."

"Nonsense." James waved it off. "I loved hearing about your job." He gestured for her to enter. "I'm glad you found something you enjoy so much. I wish I could say the same about my job . . ." His voice trailed off.

As she passed through the door, Rachel caught a tinge of sadness lingering on his face. The door closed behind them, shutting the topic off with it.

CHAPTER TEN

Peering over the top of her menu, Rachel asked, "What do you usually get here? Besides the mango sticky rice."

"Honestly," James gazed across the table at her, making her body buzz, "I always order way more than I can possibly eat because I can't decide—then I end up taking most of it home."

Rachel laid her menu flat against the table, leaning toward him. She spoke with a serious tone. "I think you just figured out my secret love language."

James scratched his head. "Huh?"

"My secret love language is food—and lots of it." Rachel stared at him, daring him to argue.

James gave a hearty laugh. "Mine too." His finger ran across the menu. "Since that's the case, we need this entire side of the menu. Don't you think?" He looked at her for confirmation.

Rachel shifted, leaning closer. His manly scent danced in between them, making her dizzy. "Absolutely..." She scanned the list of items. "It should hold us until at least tomorrow."

"Then it's settled." James closed his menu, glancing around for the server. He motioned him over.

The server came over, and James did exactly what he promised to do. He ordered half the menu.

Straightening his silverware, James couldn't believe the turning of the tide. He was out. With Rachel. On a date. And she was everything, EVERYTHING, he imagined she would be: funny, gracious, and passionate. And man, did she look cute in scrubs. She tugged at the hem of her shirt and fiddled with her hair. Hair he imagined plunging his fingers into, allowing the silky strands to glide through them.

The food started to arrive. Plates and plates of it.

Rachel nearly spit out her Pad Thai when the server swung around again with another platter of food. "There's more!" Wide-eyed, she exclaimed, "I think we've run out of space."

Anxiously, the server scanned the packed two-top table. Even with the skillful nudging of this and that, there simply wasn't enough space. James guessed he had gone to a little bit of an extreme in his attempt to please Rachel. But her wish was his command. If her love language was food, then he planned on buying stock in it.

James wiped his face with his napkin as the server hovered by their table with two huge plates of food. "Could you maybe put the rest of the food in to-go boxes?"

The server rolled his eyes. "Fine, whatever," he mumbled loudly under his breath. Pivoting on his foot, he huffed and puffed away from the table.

Rachel giggled. "Oh, I think he likes us." Her voice was laced with double meaning.

"I'm sure we can expect an invitation to his wedding," James grinned as he speared another piece of spicy broccoli, shoving the piece into his mouth.

Smiling, with fork in mid-air, Rachel added, "No doubt, he'll ask you to be a groomsman." Then she took a bite.

"Naturally," James smirked. "I might even get bumped up to best man before the night is over."

Their eyes locked. He didn't look away, not even as the sound of his heart rang in his ears or when his middle did a somersault. He was in trouble. Rachel was as enchanting as he remembered. Funny and witty, with equal parts intelligence and humor. During the entire dinner, he hadn't thought about work once.

No doubt his inbox was piling up, while emails would be marked urgent. He didn't care, not now, not tonight, when he was here with his dream girl, eating Thai food and exchanging flirty banter.

"Have I told you about my roommate, Amber, yet?" asked Rachel.

James shook his head. "No, not yet. What about her?"

"I'm pretty sure she hates me." Rachel exhaled.

"How could anyone ever hate you?" James reached out and ran a finger across her hand. "You might be the nicest person I've ever met."

"I appreciate you saying that, but it's true she doesn't like me." Rachel fiddled with the napkin in her lap. "Amber has this whole deadpan thing she does. Half the time I'm unsure if she's being serious or openly mocking me." She threw up a hand and shrugged. "But I'll figure her out some day."

They continued to chat and eat. The evening passed quicker than he wanted.

Rachel licked her full, luscious lips slowly, while gently patting her stomach. "I don't know how much more I can eat." Then she scooted her noodles around with her fork.

James set down his fork, taking a drink. "I daresay I've reached capacity too." The packed table still held enough food for a family of four.

Gnawing on a fingernail, Rachel asked, "What are we going to do with all this food? This isn't even all of it."

James waved a hand over the food. "No worries." He leaned back in his chair while Rachel tracked his movements. He tugged at his shirt collar, acutely aware he liked having Rachel look at him like *that*. "I'll have my new best friend pack it all up, and you can take it home."

Rachel laughed, then leaned forward, resting her elbow on the table to cradle her chin. "I can't take all of this." Her eyes widened as she peered at all the food. "It's way too much."

"Sure you can," James smirked. "You can share it with your roommate, Amber."

"True." Rachel nodded. "Food might be the way to win Amber over."

"Food always works." James winked. "You said so yourself."

Rachel shifted in her chair while running a finger around in a circle over the top of her glass. "Are you sure you don't want half?"

"Nah." James waved it off. "I'm good. You take it. I need to head back to work and don't have anywhere to store it."

James glanced at his watch for the first time since they sat down. His heart halted to a stop. It was almost ten. The two of them had been there for almost three hours. His blood pressure began a steady rise as anxiety pulsated through his veins. Acid bubbled its way up his throat. Swallowing, he forced the burning bile back down. With several documents that needed to be sent out asap, he wondered how he had been so nonchalant and irresponsible.

"I—" James stammered, shifting in his seat. "I didn't realize how long we'd been here. I need to get going. Geez . . ." He plunged his fingers through his hair, glancing around for the waiter. He made eye contact with him and waved him over.

While the waiter approached, he shoved his hand into his pocket. Pulling out his wallet, he found his credit card, holding it out to the waiter. "Here, do you mind ringing us up right away? I'm in a hurry." James glanced at the table full of food. "And while you're at it, could you please bring us a bunch of to-go boxes?"

"Of course, *no* problem," the waiter muttered under his breath. He left with James's credit card.

Rachel sat up straight, grabbing her purse. "Sorry, I didn't mean to keep you." She zipped it closed and placed it over her shoulder.

James wasn't thinking straight, not with his workload landing square on his shoulders, making his neck ache and chest tight. Quickly, he catalogued everything he needed to do before midnight. Only by pure luck could he accomplish all of it. He peered past Rachel, searching for signs of the waiter, hoping for his speedy return.

If James walked fast enough, or even better, caught a cab, he could make it back to his office with an hour and a half left to get out the needed document. The other side of the deal was expecting the changes by midnight. It wasn't ideal, but he hoped it would be enough time. Though the evening had been every-thing he could have dreamed of, his mind rapidly entered survival mode.

Abruptly James stood, pushing in his chair. "I'm sorry. I need to go." *Don't panic. It'll be okay. You'll get the work done in time. Calm down.* He wanted badly to believe it was possible, but the sinking feeling in his gut made it hard. "I have a document that needs to be sent out before midnight."

"Oh, okay." Rachel stood too. Wringing her hands together, she shuffled her feet. "I . . . I . . ." She took one glance at him, then darted her eyes away from him.

The waiter returned with his credit card, a receipt, and a bunch of boxes. James grabbed the check and signed it, leaving a large tip for their obviously longer than normal use of the table and extra food deliveries.

Rachel took a few of the boxes and began shoveling the

remaining food into to-go boxes. "James, you go." She waved him off without looking over at him, which he knew wasn't a good sign. "I live in the opposite direction of your work. You're obviously in a hurry. I'll pack up the rest of it. *Go.*" Closing the first box of food, she took the next one off the stack and scraped off the next plate of food into it.

This wasn't the way James wanted the night to end. If anything, he imagined walking her home, letting his fingers interlock with hers, while she leaned into his arm. That's what he longed for, not this. But duty called like it always did.

Rubbing the back of his neck, James replied, "I can't do that to you. It's okay . . ." He forced himself to take a deep breath. *It'll be okay. Don't spiral.* "I can take you home."

"No way." Rachel continued to box up food without looking up. "Go. I'll see you again soon. Thanks for a great night."

James knew he was making a huge mistake. A mistake big enough it might cost him his chance with Rachel. Peering down at his watch, he checked the time: 10:22. He wouldn't make it to his office till 10:45. If he took Rachel home, then caught a taxi to his office, he'd be lucky to make it there by 11:15. The mere thought made his blood pressure simmer to near boiling point. The choice was made. James didn't want to be fired. If he blew off his impending midnight deadline, he probably would be.

James hesitated, already hating himself. "Are you sure you don't mind?"

"Yes." Rachel glanced up at him, meeting his eyes for the first time. Her lips formed a forced crooked smile. "Now go, get out of here."

His stomach twisted in knots, James replied, "Thanks for a great night. I'll see you soon."

Rachel gave a slight nod while moving to place some of the boxes of food into one of the plastic bags.

With nothing left to do, James left. When his feet hit the pavement outside of the restaurant, he started a dead sprint back to his office. His labored breathing made it hard for him to think about anything other than sending out the necessary document with its needed changes. A three-hour dinner date evaporated into thin air with a snap. Rachel became a blur, along with everything else except for the need to save his job.

CHAPTER ELEVEN

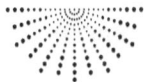

Lightly knocking on the door of her patient's room, Rachel waited for the familiar "enter" reply. Once she heard it, she pushed open the door, entering the labor and delivery room.

"How are we doing, Eliza?" Rachel went to the sink to wash her hands before putting on gloves.

She glanced over her shoulder, taking in the full view of her patient. Eliza looked extra ghastly. Her hair was pulled up haphazardly into a messy bun, while moisture made her forehead glisten under the overly harsh fluorescent lights. The woman had only been in labor for a few hours, but she wanted to have a natural birth. Rachel had never given birth, only helped others, but she was always amazed by the women who willingly chose to give natural childbirth.

"Please, tell me I've progressed some since the last time you checked me." Eliza's voice was strained, and she shifted uncomfortably in her hospital bed. Her husband, Nick, grabbed her hand. Eliza glanced at the monitor that was tracking her contractions. "These contractions . . ."

Closing her eyes, Eliza stopped speaking and squeezed her husband's hand. A long, deep moan escaped her mouth. Maybe she was entering the transition period? Rachel went over to the monitor, scanning through the information on her last several contractions. Eliza was making progress, but the contractions were still five minutes apart.

Once the wave of the contraction was over, clearly exasperated, Eliza sighed. "How much longer am I going to have to do this?"

Biting down on her bottom lip, Rachel replied, "Let me check you, and I can see how dilated you are. Last time I checked, you were at a five. Halfway there." Her voice came off overly cheerful, even to herself.

"I can't do this," Eliza moaned, slamming her eyes shut. "I'm regretting not getting an epidural. Is it too late to get one?"

Not knowing how to respond, Rachel chose to pivot the conversation away from pain management. "Can you scoot to the end of the bed so I can examine you?"

Eliza obeyed.

"Let's see where you are at." Rachel examined Eliza. "Do you want the good news or the bad news?" She stripped the gloves from her hands, tossing them into the trash.

"What?" A confused look crossed her face as she eyed Nick for support.

Both peered back at Rachel with anxiety-ridden faces.

Rachel popped a hip and rested her hand on it. "You won't have time to change your mind and get an epidural."

Eliza attempted to sit up. "I won't?"

Rachel grinned. "You, my dear, are at a ten. You're in the home stretch. I'm going to find the doctor because you're ready to push."

Eliza gripped the hospital bed railing as another contraction came. "AHHH!" she screamed.

"Remember your breathing, honey," added Nick as a total look of horror overtook his face.

"You—AHHH," Eliza wailed. Slowly, the contraction ended.

With labored breathing, Eliza spit out, "You try breathing normal when your abdomen is being sliced apart with a thousand knives." Her tone was so icy it sent a chill down Rachel's spine.

"I'll be right back." Rachel moved to the exit. "We'll get this show on the road."

Rachel beelined to the nurse's station. Luckily, the doctor on-call was Dr. Grayson. She didn't have to search far because he was chatting with Ellie when she approached. Ellie and Dr. Grayson stopped speaking when she stopped in front of them.

Breathless, Rachel said, "Dr. Grayson, the patient in room eight is ready to push."

"Let's do this thing." Dr. Grayson slammed his hand on top of the nurse's station. "I'm ready. It's been a slow night, and I've been waiting my entire shift for something to happen."

Dr. Grayson took off down the corridor.

Ellie laughed, glancing at her watch. "It looks like the patient will deliver before your shift ends."

"I sure hope so." Rachel backed away from the station. "The mother is doing the birth *au naturel*. I'll talk to you after she delivers. What time are you off?"

"I only started an hour ago," Ellie called out to her. "I'm here all night."

Rachel nodded, then pivoted back around, jogging to catch up with Dr. Grayson. He was already entering the delivery room.

The rest of the birth passed in a blur. Once Eliza started to push, everything happened quickly. A fast secession of rapid actions, and the baby boy was safely delivered. Once Rachel confirmed both mom and baby were doing great, she wandered back to the nurses' station to update Eliza's chart.

Finding an empty chair, Rachel sat down at the nurses' station. A mostly quiet evening gave her some needed time to fill out charts before the end of her shift. Of course, Rachel didn't want too much downtime. When she had time to think, she only thought about how James hadn't contacted her since their dinner date. This bummed her out. Royally. It shouldn't have come as a surprise James hadn't called, not after his abrupt departure. Sure, he blamed it on a sudden work assignment. But she had been ghosted before and knew sometimes things didn't go as well as you thought. And you didn't get the joy of figuring that out until several days went by with the guy *not* contacting you. Perhaps Rachel hadn't seen the signs he had wanted to leave earlier?

Rachel wrote the last of her notes on Eliza's chart, closing it and adding it to the proper pile. She picked up the next one in the stack.

Ellie appeared out of nowhere, joining her at the nurses' station. "You have any big plans for tonight?"

Rachel flinched, peering over at her. "No, not really." Pulling her gaze away from Ellie, she continued filling in the needed patient information. "I've got nothing planned."

Ellie let out an exasperated sigh. "That makes two of us." She folded her arms, leaning her back against the nurses' station. "I'm not off till midnight. No wonder I'm single. The only people wandering around the city at that hour are total weirdos."

Laughing, Rachel nodded in agreement. "Sad but oh so true." Rachel clicked her pen closed, adding the chart to the appropriate box. "I plan on eating take-out in my comfiest pj's. I can't wait."

Ellie raised her eyebrow. "It's only six!" she exclaimed. "My thinking doesn't apply to you."

Rachel agreed, but she was tired, and her bed was calling her name. Closing her eyes for a moment, she pinched the bridge of her nose. "But I'm finishing an eighteen-hour shift. One of the other nurses started vomiting and had to leave early. I picked up the second half. I can't refuse the overtime pay."

Ellie shifted, dropping her folded arms. "I see. It makes sense. Are you still saving for that trip to Barcelona?"

"Every dime I can," Rachel added cheerfully. All this hard work was going to pay off someday. She was working toward a goal, and it helped her stay motivated. "I'm going to Barcelona—no matter what. Even if I work myself into the ground trying to save for it."

Her mom was supposed to go with her, but recently she had commented to Rachel that her traveling days were over. Rachel would need to rope someone into going with her. Maybe Ellie could join her? Or Haley? The details didn't matter. Even if she went alone, the beautiful architecture from Gaudi and the Mediterranean Sea were calling her name.

"I'm impressed. I never manage to save money. You deserve that trip." Ellie stood straight, pushing herself away from the nurses' station. "I need to make the rounds." She pivoted to leave. "Hey, you ever call that high school hottie, James?"

Rachel rolled her eyes. "Do you know how bad that sounds? Sounds like I'm after some underaged kid, not someone my own age."

Ellie laughed. "You knew what I meant. So?"

Rachel stood too. "Crashed and burned." She walked in the direction Ellie was headed. "He ghosted me."

"Ahh . . . I'm sorry to hear that." Ellie furrowed her brows. "I had a good feeling about him."

Rachel shrugged. "Me too." She was too tired to elaborate. Her head was pulsating, and all she wanted to do was curl up on her couch and lounge until bedtime.

The two said their goodbyes when Ellie entered her patient's room. Rachel continued to the elevators in a blur. Though she was exhausted, her mind wandered back to James. She kept going through the night, trying to figure out where she had gone wrong, looking for hidden clues she should've picked up on but didn't. The conversation had easily flowed between them, and Rachel had found him to be a great listener. There had to be some fatal character flaw in herself that had doused his interest in her.

Lost in thought, she exited the elevator. Striding across the lobby in a blurry haze, Rachel didn't spot James until he appeared right in front of her.

Her jaw dropped. "James?" Rachel shifted her purse. Staring back at him, she blinked. "What are you doing here? How long have you been here?"

Shoving his hands in his pockets, James raised his shoulders. "I got off unexpectedly early from work and decided to come by and see if I might bump into you."

"Oh." Rachel folded her arms. "Okay."

James reached out and lightly touched her on her forearm. "I'm sorry about abruptly leaving our dinner the other night."

Rachel paused, unmoving. James removed his hand.

Shaking her head, Rachel moved toward the exit. "It's fine, James." Speaking over her shoulder, Rachel picked up her pace. James lengthened his stride to remain in step with her. "We had a nice dinner. Let's leave it at that."

"No, I don't want to." James swiped at his glistening brow. "It was more than just a dinner for me."

Rachel crossed through the sliding glass doors to the outside. The summer air engulfed her with its tangy, sticky balm. Practically stifling, she tossed her hair over her shoulder as sweat instantly gathered at the nape of her neck and temples.

"Why didn't you call or text me?" Her voice cracked, revealing how vulnerable she really was, and Rachel hated it. Shaking her head, Rachel continued down the sidewalk toward the subway station, refusing to glance over at James. From the corner of her eye, she saw he was maintaining her pace. She continued, "It takes like two seconds to do that. I don't buy it."

"You don't understand," James pleaded. "I left in such a hurry, I failed to get your number."

The realization stopped Rachel in her tracks. James almost tripped on her heels. He had given her *his* business card the night of their reunion. She had never called. Then he left their date in such a rush, the two hadn't ever exchanged numbers.

Dang, James wasn't lying. The pieces of the puzzle all fell into place.

Slowing her walk to a crawl, Rachel mulled over everything. Gnawing on the inside of her cheek, she asked, "How did you even find out where I worked?"

"You told me you worked around the corner from me." James met her gaze and held it.

The bustling sounds of the city became silenced. In the busy and crowded city, it was only her and James.

He cleared his throat. "Luckily," James continued, "there's only one hospital within walking distance of my office, so I took a chance it was the right place."

"Why did you leave so abruptly?" Rachel sputtered out, unable to shake the feeling of rejection embedded inside of her. "I thought we were having a nice time."

James took one step closer to her. "I was having the best time."

He reached for her hand, allowing their fingers to slightly intertwine. A swimming sensation filled her middle. She studied his jawline and windswept hair. They stood there for a moment, staring at one another.

James continued, "I wasn't lying when I said I had a document that needed to be sent out before midnight." He lowered his voice. "My entire career hung in the balance. It was my fault I'd lost track of time. The time passed so quickly, I was shocked when I finally checked my watch. Then the panic set in, and I couldn't think straight. I left in such a hurry. I apologize."

Rachel nodded. "Does your job always cause you problems when you date?"

James glanced away.

"I get the work thing." Rachel rubbed at her temple with her free hand. "I work a lot, too, but—there has to be more to the story."

James released his hand from hers, wiping it down his face. "I

... I ..." He stumbled over his words while he rubbed the back of his neck. "I haven't been very lucky in love. I had a pretty serious relationship a few years back. I thought I was going to marry her, but she ended it out of the blue. It left me broken and scared of trying again. I threw myself into work to forget about the whole thing. It's my coping mechanism. Work is the one great distraction in my life. In some ways, it's all I really have, but I want that to change. I don't want to live this way anymore."

A million questions sprung up in her mind. "I see." Rachel tried to think of something else to say, but she was afraid of pressing him further.

His expression softened, making his jaw loosen. "Can we have a do over? This Saturday, I want to take you on a proper date ... that's if you'll give me another chance."

Rachel paused, closing her eyes for a moment. Could she trust James a second time? Or was the whole thing a colossal waste of time? Before she had time to overthink the possibility of heartbreak, she replied, "I'm actually free this Saturday."

"Perfect," James grinned. "I'll pick you up at noon."

"Noon?" Rachel forced a laugh. "A day date?" It didn't exactly scream a recipe for romance. Day dates were usually reserved for people you weren't sure about.

James grinned. "I've the perfect place to take you, and it's better to go during the day."

Fiddling with her loose strands of hair, Rachel tucked them behind her ears. "And where might this be?" She raised an eyebrow.

James wrapped his arm around her shoulders, giving them a squeeze. "It's a surprise. I'll tell you when I pick you up."

Playfully, Rachel nudged him with her elbow. "I hate surprises. Just tell me."

James laughed. He shook his head, making a zip-his-lips motion. "But don't you worry. I promise we'll have a good time." He dropped his arm from her shoulders, pulling out his cell phone. "Now, let me get your cell phone number and address so this whole mix up doesn't happen again."

The two exchanged numbers and parted in their opposite directions. Rachel turned back around, peeking, as he melted into the sea of people heading down the street. Wistfully, she sighed, hopeful once more. Until Saturday.

CHAPTER TWELVE

Climbing up the stairs from the subway stop, James double-checked the address of Rachel's apartment in the East Village. After a short walk, he arrived at her apartment. Then he huffed and puffed his way to her fifth story walk up. Landing in front of her door, he leaned over with his hands on his knees to regain his breath.

Once his labored breathing returned to normal, James knocked lightly on her apartment door. A few moments later, the door swung open.

An unfamiliar woman answered. "Hello." With a hand on her hip and one still on the door, she eyed him suspiciously. Her voice was gruff. "What do you want?"

James checked the address again on his phone, confirmed it was the correct apartment number, then peered back at the woman with bleached blonde hair and bright red lipstick. "Is Rachel home?" he asked.

The woman rolled her eyes, pushing open the door the rest of the way. She left him lingering in front of the door, speaking over her shoulder. "She's home." Her voice was borderline between monotone and annoyed. "Rachel," she shrieked, "some guy is here for you." Then she promptly plopped herself back down on the sofa and unmuted the TV.

Unsure of what to do, James closed the door behind him, waiting in front of the closed door. The one room was a small living and dining room combo. A few strides in either direction, you'd be able to touch either wall. Again, this was Manhattan. His apartment wasn't big either, but he was suddenly grateful he no longer had to share it with a roommate.

James forced himself to start a conversation. "So . . ." He clenched his hands into fists at the side of his body to fight off the anxiety he felt surrounding his date. "Are you and Rachel roommates?"

Deadpan, she turned her attention from the TV to him. "The man's a genius." It came out as a snarl. "Yes, Einstein," she muttered. "I'm Amber, her roommate."

Shuffling his feet, James pushed his hands into his pockets. "Okay . . . that's nice." He was at a loss for words, so he didn't attempt to make any more conversation.

Clearly, Rachel hadn't hit the roommate jackpot. She had mentioned before how Amber was challenging to live with, but being a nurse and all, he imagined her options for affordable places to live in the city were limited.

After long moments of awkward silence, Rachel arrived in the living room wearing a light floral summer dress, smiling. "Hey, you." Rachel glanced between him and Amber lounging on the sofa with the TV on at an unbearably high volume. Head tilting toward Amber, she slowly said, "I see you met Amber."

James forced a smile. "I sure did."

A moment of understanding passing between them. Rachel smirked. Her lips did a cute twitching motion.

Rachel strode the few steps to the two-person dining table, grabbing her purse off the top. "I'm ready." Rachel slung it over her shoulder, then spoke in the direction of Amber. "Amber, I'm off. See you later."

Amber didn't look over from the TV, but mumbled a goodbye.

James bid farewell to Amber too, allowing Rachel to exit first. Once the door closed, the tight, intimate space in front her apartment forced their bodies to brush up against each other. Rachel side stepped. He caught the scent of her perfume, making his nostrils flare. *Oh, boy. I am in trouble.* His knees wobbled a tad. Rachel looked beautiful *and* smelled good. His mind became a muddled mess while Rachel walked to the stairs and started down them. Half tripping on the first step, James followed behind her.

On the stairs, James said, "Amber seems . . . interesting."

Glancing over her shoulder and up at him, Rachel laughed. "That's a nice way of putting it." She pivoted forward, continuing down. "Amber is a total grouch and recluse. She works from home and barely leaves the apartment. But the rent is way below market value, so I deal with it." She shrugged.

"Makes sense," James added. "Besides, I'm sure you have the personality to handle her."

Exiting the stairwell, the balmy summer air engulfed them. James tugged at his shirt collar, hoping he didn't put Rachel off by sweating through his shirt. Being noon, the sun menacingly glared down at them. He tried to remember if he had put on sunblock or not. His pocket vibrated. James slipped his phone from his pocket. Scanning the incoming email, nothing appeared urgent. He put his phone on silent so it wasn't a distraction and put it back into his pocket.

Rachel lingered on the sidewalk in front of her apartment, fluffing her hair in a way that made his mind run wild through myriad fantasies. He must have been staring, because she cleared her throat, awakening him from his daze.

Popping a hip, Rachel asked, "So, where are you taking me, mystery man?" Her eyes twinkled back at him.

James shifted his weight. "I thought we could take the Staten Island Ferry." He thrust one hand into his pocket. "It has a great view of the Statue of Liberty and the city skyline. Then after we get there, we can eat. If you aren't sick of me by then, there's a lighthouse museum I thought might be interesting to check out." He hoped she found his planned-out date acceptable, because he had enlisted the help of Ryan to plan it.

"Wow." Rachel's jaw dropped. "I'm impressed. You're a guy who knows how to date." She playfully hit him on the arm, making him take a step. "You've been holding out on me."

His cheeks warmed. James rubbed the back of his neck. "I wouldn't say I'm a guy who knows how to date—unless you count one date in like a year." James locked eyes with Rachel.

Silence followed, hovering between them, making his heart hammer and temples pulsate. *This was bad. You are revealing too much too soon. You might scare her off.*

Tilting her head to the side, a slow smirk crept across her face. Rachel made a tsk sound with her tongue. "The ladies have no idea what they're missing." Her voice was soft and velvety.

His nerves evaporated into thin air as Rachel put him at ease.

James motioned in the direction they should go. The two fell into step with one another. Their arms brushed against one another a few times as they squeezed closer together on the busy sidewalk. Feeling bold, on the next bumping of their arms, he reached for her hand, allowing his fingers to interlock with hers. Rachel didn't pull her hand away, instead giving his hand a reassuring squeeze. Being with her was perfectly intoxicating. He recklessly abandoned any of his previous inhibitions.

After walking for a few minutes, James asked, "How about you? Does your schedule allow you to date a lot?"

"Umm . . ." Gnawing down on her bottom lip, Rachel hesitated. A slight summer breeze picked up, a welcome relief to the already hot, muggy air. "I . . . I . . ." She stammered.

James quickly added, "You don't have to answer. It really isn't any of my business. I was only curious. I know you work a lot too. With me, it's hard to carve out time to go out."

Her demeanor softened, the worry lines on her forehead smoothed out. Rachel squeezed his hand again. "But you found time today."

"Yes, but you're different. You've always been this unattainable woman in my world." James's body was pulsating, making his skin awaken. Being here with Rachel, a longtime dream and fantasy all wrapped up into one, was doing all sorts of funky things to him. He tried not to think ten steps ahead, but instead he forced himself to live in the moment. "I'll always make time for you."

"Thanks?" The word came out as a cross between a question and a statement. "I mean, no pressure, right?" Rachel gave a nervous laugh, diverting her gaze from him to the sidewalk.

"I'm sorry." James ran his free hand through his hair. "Let me rephrase that. I enjoy your company. And because I enjoy your company, I'll find a way, even with my long work hours, to be with you."

Her cheeks tinged pink, and Rachel gave a small nod of acknowledgement. They continued toward the ferry in silence. As the Staten Island Terminal came into view, James wondered if the day would be filled with these awkward exchanges and not the easy conversation, they shared at the Thai restaurant. He was to blame. Being around Rachel made him jittery. Right out of the gate, he was speaking too much and revealing more than he should. James made a note to himself to be more careful.

In front of the ferry landing, Rachel ended the silence. "James, I'm glad you chose to spend your day with me. You're way different from any of the men I've dated in the past." Her voice cracked. "You're a nice guy. It will take me some getting used to."

James reached out, running a hand up and down her arm. "Now, that's just sad."

His gaze picked up the sadness lingering in her eyes. He saw it all there, years of dating and re-dating different men in her life.

Men who undoubtedly had disappointed her with broken promises and unfaithfulness.

"I know." Rachel exhaled, making her shoulders droop. "But it's the truth. It's why I am leery of dating again, to put myself out there. I don't want to regret it later when I get my heart broken."

James gave her hand a squeeze, then reached out, tucking some loose strands of hair behind her ear. "I hope to change all of that for you." His hand lingered a tad too long by her ear. He forced himself to pull away.

Slowly, her lips curled up into a wide smile, making his middle a fiery baking mess.

"I hope you can too." Rachel kissed him quickly on the cheek. "I'm glad we have today. I'm glad I'm here with you."

———

Rachel and James boarded the ferry, finding a place outside against the railing. After a minute, the ferry pulled away from the dock. While cruising, they took in the city skyline as it headed toward Ellis Island.

Rachel turned, leaning against the railing, and faced James. "Why did you move to New York City?" she asked.

James moved closer to her, gripping the railing with one hand as he leaned in. Rachel could smell his tangy aftershave and minty breath. *Why did he have to smell so exhilaratingly good?* His closeness made goosebumps run rampant down her spine. He didn't break their gaze. *This isn't good. He can't look at me that way. I won't be able to resist. Do I want to resist?* She gulped, waiting for him to answer.

"I had to get out of that town." James's jaw tightened, and he glanced out at the water. The words hovered between them, pulsating in the very air they breathed. "I hated it in Cloverton." He didn't continue, instead he tightened his grip on the railing, making his knuckles turn white.

Rachel had a million little questions, and she wondered where to even begin. Unlike him, though she left their hometown for NYC, she didn't want to close the door completely on Cloverton. Her parents and brother still lived there. Someday she might hope to resettle there to raise children. Yes, Cloverton was small and had its problems, but it didn't change the fact it was home. Was Cloverton home? She questioned her thinking. New York fit her perfectly, and she loved everything about this city. Her thoughts were all jumbled.

"What was so bad about it?" Rachel watched as they passed Ellis Island, continuing toward the Statue of Liberty.

James exhaled, shaking his head. "What's good about it?" He glanced over at her, meeting her gaze, challenging her to prove what she believed.

Rachel shifted, leaning on him. She wrapped her hands around his elbow. "AHH—there's a lot of good things about Cloverton, like the fall harvest carnival or the spring fling. Also, it has all those cute shops that dot Main Street. And at the public library—the librarian, Laura, knows everyone's name. The Watering Hole has the best burgers in town . . ."

His sculpted biceps tightened under her touch. "The only burgers in town," James mumbled. "I'm still not convinced." He shook his head. "There's nothing there for me. Nothing I want to remember."

The silence which followed was humongous. So wide and so grand, she wondered what he was refusing to divulge. Instead of letting it ruin the day, Rachel changed the subject. "The Statue of Liberty always looks more impressive from far away, don't you think?"

Slowly, James patted the top of her hand around his elbow. He tilted his head, resting it on top of hers. "I'd have to completely agree." His words made her neck tickle. "It's way more impressive from here than up close. It looks spectacular from a plane."

Her cheeks warmed. Temples pulsating, Rachel managed to say, "I'm glad we can agree on something."

James nodded. The tense exchange from before floated away. He wrapped his arm around her shoulders. Rachel snuggled against him and contentment filled her being. Being there with him, staring out at the glistening water, pushed the exchange about Cloverton far away. No need to worry about all that right now. The two stayed there wrapped up in each other's arms, watching in blissful peace as the ferry moved toward Staten Island.

Rachel didn't want the ferry ride to end, but soon it landed at Staten Island. The other passengers made their way toward the exit. James slipped his arm from her shoulders down the length of her arm until his fingers interlocked with hers.

In a daze, she followed him off the ferry.

Once back on solid ground, James said, "There's a pizza place only a short walk from here." He looked at her for approval. "Is that okay?"

With a bright smile, Rachel gave his hand an encouraging squeeze. "Sounds fantastic."

Over lunch, the conversation flowed. James had a calm presence, which put her at ease. They covered everything one could imagine, everything but Cloverton and why he didn't like it. After lunch they wandered through the lighthouse museum, Rachel caught James a few times staring at her which made the air practically crackle and sizzle. Rachel enjoyed being with James, and it made her hopeful in a way she hadn't been in a long time.

As the two boarded the ferry to head back to NYC, Rachel longed for the day to not end.

"Let's go up to the front," James said. "It has the best view of the skyline on the way back to the city."

Rachel leaned into his arm, wrapping one arm around his waist. "You lead the way."

James mirrored her movements, wrapping an arm around

her, too. He guided her through the throngs of people, and slowly they inched their way to the front of the ferry. On the horizon, the setting sun painted a beautiful backdrop of orange and yellow stretched across the sky. Only a few minutes of sunlight remained before the darkness would envelop them, and the flickering lights of the city lit up the sky. It was spectacular.

With the sun nearly gone, the heat had subsided. Rachel breathed in the cool air and sighed with contentment. "I do love it here." Leaning over the railing, she took in the vast waters before them. "All of it."

"I do too." James turned his back from the view, resting himself against the railing to face her. "I don't think I'll ever leave. I want to live here forever."

Rachel remained restrained. The words gripped her gut, making it clench tight. This might not ever work. She didn't have a future with anyone who wanted to live their entire life in NYC. Though she loved it here, she imagined all of that might change once she had a family. The thought of pushing a stroller down crowded streets, lugging groceries up and down five flights of stairs with a baby in tow, seemed horrible. Yes, at this moment, she loved living in NYC. But being here forever? It seemed unlikely. What would happen years from now when the magic of the city wore off? And she wanted *space,* which was something very hard to find in the city without being a millionaire. Yes, she was skipping too many steps ahead in her thinking, but she couldn't shake the nagging feeling trapped inside of her.

"I don't know about being here *forever.* Priorities change," Rachel stated, her eyes steady on the water. She could feel him taking her in, his gaze making her acutely aware of her hair flapping this way and that way with the wind. Finally, she turned back toward him. She blinked. "People's opinions and wants can change too."

It was the best she could manage. There was so much left unsaid, and myriad thoughts whirled around in her head.

"I understand that." His gaze found hers. Eyes locked, James unflinchingly stated, "But mine won't. I can't ever live in Cloverton again."

Tightness grew in Rachel's chest. None of this should matter, not now, when neither knew where any of this was going. Though she still found it hard to nudge away the feeling that if they dated and things progressed, then she needed to accept forever with James meant forever in NYC. The two were clearly tightly wound together, and she had no idea if she could live with that. But she shoved the worries away, closing the door and embracing the possibility of something.

"Let's not focus on any of this right now." Rachel turned, tilting her chin up toward him. "I want to enjoy this moment with you. It's been a wonderful day. I don't want anything to mess that up."

James swallowed, making his Adam's apple bob up and down. "Yeah, I know—I'm just glad . . ." He stammered. "I'm glad we had this perfect day together." He reached out and brushed her unruly hair out of her eyes, tucking the loose strands back into place. His hand lingered by her ear, cupping her neck.

Rachel's heartbeat rang in her ears as his gaze made her skin tingly. The stresses from seconds before whirled away with the breeze. All she desired was this beautiful day to end with a kiss. With the sweet summer air blowing between them, James looked to her for confirmation to move closer. Slowly, she reached up and covered his hand with her own.

"Thanks for taking me here." Her voice shook as she gulped in the sweet air. "I loved being with you."

The last streak of sunlight glistened across his face. James looked so hot. It made her temples pulsate, and Rachel found it hard to concentrate on anything but imagining his lips on hers.

James grinned. "Thanks for giving me another chance and going out with me again."

Her eyes flickered between his eyes and his lips and back again. "Happy to oblige."

Moistening his lips, James leaned in closer, and only inches remained between them. Rachel rested her hand on his chest. He was warm and steady under her palm. She blinked. With no time to process what was happening, James closed the gap, allowing his lips to glide over hers. It was all the invitation she needed.

Rachel gripped a fistful of his shirt, tugging him closer to her. He tightened his hold around her waist, deepening the kiss, making her lips tingle. Her heart tripled its speed as she felt the roughness of his stubble against her cheek. Time slowed. The apprehension about the future evaporated into thin air. On a ferry full of people, in this magical moment, it was only him and her. Kissing, for the first time, and she didn't want him to stop. Ever.

His hand traced the slope of her jaw as her lips parted, allowing his tongue to plunge inside. Whirling and twirling, the kiss took her further and further away from reality, making her forget the years of ache, the years of broken hearts and failed dreams. Here and now, with James kissing her, she believed again in the never-ending magic of what could be.

CHAPTER THIRTEEN

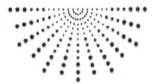

James led Rachel off the ferry, interlacing his fingers with hers. The two walked hand-in-hand back to her apartment. With the memory of their kiss lingering on his mind, he found it hard to not skip a thousand steps ahead. Kissing Rachel was a million times better than anything he ever imagined.

Then reality struck: The moment was fleeting. He hadn't checked his phone once the entire day since he put it on silent.

Releasing his hand from hers, he yanked his cell phone out of his pocket. His heart skidded to a screeching stop as he scanned the long stream of notifications for both emails and text messages on his home screen. The part between his shoulder blades pinched tight. He inhaled, halting in his tracks. Rachel stopped too.

"Everything okay?" Rachel wrung her hands together while shifting her weight.

Distracted, James hardly registered the worried look on her face. Instead, he continued to scan his piled-up messages. "Umm . . ." James scrolled some more. "Not really."

Bile bubbled up in his throat. During his blissful day with Rachel, the case he was working on had managed to crumble. By ignoring all his messages, he had created a problem so big it would likely take him the rest of the weekend to fix. It potentially might cost him his client. Rubbing his jaw raw, James's mind made lists of tasks to do when he made it back to his office. There would be consequences for his carpe diem attitude.

"I'm sorry. Anything I can do to help?" Rachel fiddled with her purse strap.

The gap between them widened, and not just physically.

He ignored her as he continued to scroll, then finally said, "Everything is a complete mess." James ran a hand down the length of his face then rubbed the back of his neck. Inhaling, he wished to settle his heart rate enough for him to think straight. He didn't need Rachel to think he was a jerk, when deep down he wasn't. "I shouldn't have stayed out so long. I need to call it a day. I have an inbox full of emails and a ton of things I neglected today. Let me finish walking you home."

James immediately regretted stating his long stream of consciousness. His words only made this worse, way worse. Though his stresses were real, he didn't need to push them off onto Rachel. She didn't deserve to be treated this way, again. Boy, he had managed to mess everything up. No wonder he was still single.

Curtly, Rachel nodded without a reply and continued in the direction of her apartment. James slid his phone back into his pocket and jogged to catch up with her. Luckily, Rachel's apartment was only a few blocks away. After dropping her off, he could take a taxi across town. He'd be pulling an all-nighter, but at this point everything was still fixable.

They walked two blocks before the light turned red, and they were forced to halt.

"I can see your work is very . . . demanding." Rachel crossed her arms, keeping her gaze on the crossing light. "I'm sorry."

James exhaled. His stomach in knots. "Unfortunately, I do have a rather demanding schedule." The pinched nerve between his shoulder blades began radiating surges of pain down his back. Again, the evening wasn't ending well. All due to his job. Desperately, he wanted to correct the course, but his mind rattled off his workload. "But trust me, I wish I could spend the rest of the evening with you."

The words must have fallen flat, because Rachel didn't look over at him. The light changed, and she moved into the crosswalk. Her apartment came into view.

"I hope you can figure out or fix whatever it is you need to." Rachel stopped in front of her apartment.

After digging around in her purse, she pulled out her keys. Climbing the few stairs up to the front door, Rachel fiddled with her keys, trying to locate the correct one. Moments ticked by in heavy silence, making his skin crawl.

James reached out, touching her lightly on her forearm. She halted in place, tracing his hand all the way up to his eyes.

He cleared his throat. "I'm sorry about being stressed about work." James forced a smile. "But I'm glad we had today together."

"It was a pleasant day." Rachel gnawed on her bottom lip while she shifted her weight. "I enjoy being around you. I probably talked too much and kept you out way longer than you planned."

Placing both of his hands on her shoulders, James stated, "You didn't keep me out too long. If I want to blow off work, that's my choice. I know the consequences."

Letting his hands glide from her shoulders, James trailed them down her arms until both of his hands interlocked with hers. He gave them a squeeze. Then James released the grip of one hand and landed it squarely on the door behind her, leaning in closer. Rachel rested her back against the door. He caught a vague scent of her perfume, making the tension in his shoulders dissipated.

Eyes locked, his temples pulsated from her gaze. James

continued, "This has been the best day *ever*, because I was with you."

A smile crept across her face, reaching all the way to her eyes. Rachel wistfully sighed. "I feel the same way."

The words swayed between them, embedding themselves firmly into his heart. Here with his dream girl, she chose to stay. Every part of him longed for the feel of her hair between his fingertips, the steady rise of his heartbeat, the fruity taste of her lip balm, and the distinct tantalizing scent radiating off her body.

"I'm glad to hear it." The words were meant to be flirty, but instead came out shaky. James was back to the boy he was in high school, terrified the pretty girl in class would reject him. Despite these past emotions, he forced himself to be courageous. He cleared his throat, gathering his nerves and placing them back in the box. "I, for one, plan on spending as much time as possible with you in the future."

Reaching out, Rachel traced a single finger along his chest, making his middle pool into a huge heaping mess.

"Really?" replied Rachel.

James gulped. "You can bet money on it."

Shifting even closer, James moved so her body was between both of his legs. With no time to think if he was being too bold in kissing her again, James placed both hands on her waist. Rachel responded instantly by gripping his shirt and heaving him against her. Their hips nearly collided with one another.

With a smirk, Rachel stated, "This time I am going to kiss *you*."

Rachel tilted her head toward his. Soon, her moistened lips glided over his, coating them with her delectable lip balm. As they dipped and dived, in and out and all around, James's mind went blank. This kiss topped the one on the ferry, which James didn't believe was possible. But her titillating aroma whirled around, tickling at his nose. His insides did a somersault.

Soon, he was transported elsewhere to a different time and place. A place where he was safe and loved. A place where the world made sense because Rachel made all the little clicks of the dial lock into the correct space. Her fingers plunged into his hair, massaging his temples. He held her steady with one arm, while the other freely laced her silky hair through his fingertips. Her fingers raked the hair around his temples in a calming, circular motion.

Breathless, James forced himself to pull away. His hand flew to his heart while he gasped for air. With each thump of his heart, his breath evened out. Once in control, he kissed her on the temple and wrapped his arms around her. Rachel snuggled up tight against him, resting her head against his chest. Both embraced each other as their hearts settled.

His phone buzzed in his pocket, breaking the spell. "I need to go." James released his arms, taking a step away. The realities of work could no longer be ignored. He still had bills to pay and simply couldn't afford to be fired. No matter how much he wanted to blow everything off.

"I know," Rachel sighed. "Call or text me, okay?" Her voice shook.

"I'll see you soon. Promise." James managed to smile.

All the while, his obligations from before came crashing down on him.

They said their goodbyes, and Rachel slipped inside.

Once she was safely inside, James glanced at his phone, and his stomach plummeted like he was on a rollercoaster. In a dream world, living free from consequences, that might have worked, but now he was one move away from getting himself fired. He clicked on his most recently missed call. Running his fingers through his hair, James listened as it rang. After a ring and a half, the person on the other side picked up.

"James, where have you been?!" Shrieked the voice on the other end.

He jogged to the edge of the sidewalk. Waving his hand, he hailed a cab. A cab abruptly stopped at the curb right in front of him, and he pulled open the door while he replied, "I'm sorry. A personal emergency."

He didn't elaborate that the so-called personal emergency was his desperate need to win over the one who got away. Sliding into the back seat of the cab, he covered the mouthpiece with his hand and told the cab driver his office address. Then he removed his hand and continued to listen to the words being spewed out at him.

The cab driver merged into traffic.

"It better have been an emergency," stated Robert, his boss, with a level of disdain that made James's blood pressure nearly explode on the spot. "Everything has hit the fan in the last five hours. There are a million different issues with the contract you drafted, and the other side is adding additional contingencies. You've got to fix this by Monday, or I don't know what is going to happen . . ." His voice trailed off. "Most likely your job will be on the line, because this isn't going to sit well with the other partners."

Everything was always at stake. Around and around he went, each deal catapulting him into harder and more complicated work. Some days, James simply wished to walk away and start all over on his own. At times, he daydreamed about opening his own law firm so he could determine the type of work and clients he wanted to take on. A new place, perhaps in a new town . . . but then he remembered the one thing he had was his reputation. If he took the risk and chose to walk away, and his clients didn't follow him, he would be left with nothing. James wasn't like other people. He didn't have a family to fall back on. There was no couch in his parents' basement he could crash on while he put the pieces of his life back together. James had nobody. No, he was on his own. And sometimes the burden felt too heavy to carry all alone.

"Calm down." James became eerily calm. The lingering memory of his kisses with Rachel made him smile. He shook his head, allowing his survival instinct to kick in. "When have I ever let you down? I'll fix it and get it done. You know I am a man of my word." His voice commanded the strength rising within him.

He wanted to add, he wouldn't sleep for forty-eight hours or even eat a full meal. The whole deal would probably take a solid decade off his life expectancy, but with years of wisdom under his belt, he knew he would come out on the other side alive. Even if he barely survived.

"I need the redraft by morning. We'll talk then." Robert didn't wait for a response. The phone went dead.

James pulled it away from his ear, glancing at the screen as it flashed from call ended to his screen saver. His stomach churned as he peered out the window of the back seat. The bright lights of the city made his temples throb as the high rises passed by in a blur. *Tonight is going to be a doozy.*

The rest of the drive to his office ticked by in a nauseous haze as he catalogued the many things he needed to fix. Next thing he knew, James had arrived at his office. Climbing out of the cab, he glanced up at the high-rise. His date with Rachel seemed like a hundred lifetimes ago. With nothing left to do, he entered the building, stiffening his back. During his entire date with Rachel, he hadn't looked at his phone once. But then he remembered their kisses, and the tightness growing between his shoulder blades loosened. Some things were worth the risk, and Rachel certainly was one of them.

CHAPTER FOURTEEN

Rachel double-checked the business card in her hand. The number on the outside of the building matched up with the one printed on the card. She slid the card back into the pocket of her pink scrubs, while attempting to balance the to-go bag in one hand and drinks in the other. It was rare to find a man with whom you could carry on a decent conversation. A man who was kind and generous, who apologized when he was wrong, and James was all those things. Rachel knew a good thing when she saw it, and she didn't plan on letting him go.

The remembrance of their shared kisses fresh in her mind, she planned on making an impression. Even if this whole idea crashed and burned, at least she could say she tried. Approaching the door, she juggled the items in her hands and reached for the door. It didn't budge. *Maybe I didn't grip it hard enough with all the stuff in my hands?* Placing the items carefully to the right of the door, she tried again, this time with both hands and full force. Nothing. The glass door shook but remained tightly locked. This wasn't part of the plan. Why hadn't she thought this part through? It was *Sunday*, obviously big business buildings like this didn't just let anyone waltz off the street and into their building.

So much for a surprise. Poof went the fantasy scenario she had played out in her mind. Rachel dug around in her purse until she located her cell phone. Pulling up James's number, she hit call. Tapping her foot, she waited for him to answer. It rang and rang until the voicemail kicked on. She clicked end. *What now?* Her mind skidded through the list of possible ways to handle the situation.

Checking the time, she only had a half hour, max, before she needed to high-tail it to work for her shift. Diving back into her purse, she fished out his business card and typed his office number into her phone.

She hit call, waiting with bated breath as it rang.

James picked up after two rings. "Hello. This is James Ripley."

"James," Rachel sputtered out. She reached down and picked back up the to-go bag and drinks in the cardboard carrier. "Are you at your office? I wanted to drop breakfast off for you before I head to work." Her voice shook, revealing her insecurity.

Maybe she had misread how well things had gone the afternoon before. Perhaps, for James, they had simply only shared a few nice kisses.

His voice rose an octave. "Really?" James asked.

"Yes." Rachel shuffled the phone at the crook of her neck. "Do you have time to come down?" Her cheeks splashed with heat.

"I'll be right down. Give me five minutes."

Rachel exhaled, loosening the tightness in her chest. She bade him farewell and slipped her phone back into her purse.

Unsure of where to wait, Rachel searched for a place to sit but didn't see anywhere to land. Instead, she shifted her weight and juggled the items in her hands until she found a more manageable way to hold them. A few minutes ticked by, and Rachel peered into the large glass wall looking into the lobby. Eventually, James appeared. He jogged across the lobby, swiping his ID card at the sensor by the door. The glass doors swung open, revealing James in the same clothes he wore yesterday. Clearly, he had worked through the night.

With slightly labored breathing, James smiled and said, "Rachel, what a pleasant surprise." His voice was warm and inviting, smoothing out the knot in the pit of her stomach.

Rachel walked all the way into the lobby. It was wide and spacious with huge elevator queues marked ten floors at a time. At the far other end of the lobby, there were metal tables and chairs next to a closed cafeteria.

She gazed at his ruffled appearance. "Have you been here all night?" Rachel adjusted the cardboard drink carrier.

"Yes." James ran a hand through his hair. "I've been here since I dropped you off, but I think I'm through the worst of it." Leaning toward her, James reached for the drink carrier. "Here, let me help you." He grabbed it, taking it from her.

"Thanks." She meekly smiled, suddenly feeling shy and self-conscious. Hopefully, her showing up at his place of employment uninvited wasn't too forward. Surely, there were dating rules somewhere she was breaking. Ones she no longer cared to follow or worry about. "I appreciate it."

James wrapped his arm around her shoulders, giving them a tiny squeeze. "This is very thoughtful of you. I don't think anyone has ever brought me something so thoughtful."

Heat spread further down her neck. Rachel averted her glance. "I doubt that's true. It's only breakfast."

"Nonsense. It means a lot. Thanks." Quickly, James kissed her on her temple. "You're in your scrubs . . . are you coming or going to work?"

Rachel pushed back her sleeve, revealing her watch. "I'm heading to work. I only have ten minutes." She ran a hand over the top of her head. "Then I've got to dash to the hospital to start a twelve-hour shift."

James's eyes widened. "Geez. Sounds like my work schedule. Here—" He motioned toward the metal tables and chairs at the far edge of the lobby. "Let's sit over there for a few minutes. I've been up all night trying to fix a ton of problems. I was just about to call to order some food. But you luckily beat me to it."

They made their way toward the table and chairs, sitting in seats across from each other. Rachel opened the paper to-go bag and took out the breakfast burritos, handing one to James.

Rachel paused. "Hopefully, you like breakfast burritos." She gnawed on the inside of her cheek.

James grinned. "My favorite. Thanks." He peeled back the paper from the top of the burrito. "I left in such a hurry yesterday. I haven't had a chance to call or text you." He reached across the table with his free hand to find hers, giving it a squeeze. "I haven't stopped thinking about what a great time I had yesterday with you."

Her middle pooled with warmth. No doubt her rosy complexion was a dead giveaway to her mutual feelings. "I had a great time too. Here, there's salsa as well." Rachel took the little plastic cups of salsa out of the paper bag, setting them on the table. "I like the salsa verde, but I grabbed a variety of kinds. I wasn't sure if you did hot salsa or not."

Her heart hammered, and Rachel wiped her hands back and forth over the top of her thighs. Being this close to James made her skittish. Apparently, it wasn't all in her head. He had confirmed yesterday meant something. This part of dating was a fine dance, where both were showing their best selves. Then months later, when the magic wore off, they'd be able to see if this thing between them would work long term.

"I love hot salsa. I practically drown all my food in hot sauce." James doused the top of his burrito with the hottest salsa before he took a bite. He swallowed, pointing to his mouth he said, "Mm. This is delicious."

Rachel grabbed her burrito, peeling the paper back. "It's my favorite place. Luckily, it's right around the corner from my apartment building. The best part," her voice trailed off as she poured the green salsa on the top, "it's open twenty-four hours. After I get off a long shift at random hours, I always know if I'm hungry, I can stop there to grab a burrito before heading home."

"It sounds like my kind of place." James continued to eat. "And it's delicious."

They ate for a while in contented silence.

After Rachel took a few more bites of her burrito, she asked, "How much longer are you going to have to work?" She raised an eyebrow as she took in his noticeably gruff and tired appearance. Though his five o'clock shadow looked good on him, she knew he probably felt differently. "I mean, you haven't slept since yesterday."

James sighed, shaking his head. "I'll work until tonight. I think I've managed to skate by this time. And by 'skate by,' I mean I fixed the thing that only I can do." He crumpled up the empty burrito wrapper, tossing it into the trash can next to him. "I'll probably have to power through today and crash tonight."

"Is this how your job always is?" Rachel finished her burrito. "Is it always so . . . *stressful?*"

Leaning back in his chair, James put his hands behind his head. "Unfortunately, yes." He shrugged. "I wish it was different, but that's the job."

Rachel wondered if his previous relationships had fizzled out due to his work schedule. One never wanted to be second fiddle. But Rachel understood how someone's career could be their identity. She imagined James's career was where he proved his worth. He didn't have a family, so of course it had become his everything. But she pushed all her thoughts away. She didn't want to worry about his demanding work hours right now.

"My job can be stressful, too." Rachel gathered up her trash and tossed it. "I, too, must support myself in a very expensive city, which means I pick up every shift I can get. I guess we'll see if either of us will really have time to spend with each other. I mean . . ." Her cheeks burned at her misstep, and Rachel wrung her hands together under the table. Somehow, she had managed to jump ten steps ahead. They had only gone on two dates, and here she was declaring they had a future. *Yikes. Smooth, real smooth.*

Flustered, Rachel abruptly stood. "I need to go. I'm going to be late." She strode toward the exit, feeling vulnerable. Why did she always do this? Feeling too much too soon.

James jogged to catch up with her. "Rachel, wait." He arrived next to her. "I know we both work long hours, and our schedules might not always line up. But I want to see you again, and I'll do everything within my means to make it happen."

A few steps from the door, Rachel halted. She pivoted, facing him. "Do you really mean that?" Her voice softened.

"Absolutely." James ran a hand through his hair, then rubbed it at the back of his neck. "I want to date you, Rachel. In fact, I've been waiting years to do just that. Now that you're in my life, I have zero intention of letting myself mess this up."

Her jaw dropped. Rachel shuffled her feet and wondered how to respond, wondered if she should take the leap of faith and reveal her feelings, too. She stammered, "I want to spend time with you too."

Grinning, James swiped his badge at the sensor, making the doors open. Rachel stepped outside. Lingering, she glanced back at him.

Tugging her toward him, James wrapped his arms around her. Rachel melted into his hard, chiseled arms, resting her cheek against his chest. Her nostrils flared from his manly scent. Heat smoldered in her belly. Rachel pulled away enough to gaze up at him, and James brushed a few strands of hair out of her eyes.

"When will I see you again?" asked James.

Rachel rested her hand against his chest, fiddling with the collar of his shirt. "You'll see me whenever you plan something." Her pulse quickened. "The ball is in your court. I brought you breakfast burritos after all."

James traced the outline of her chin with a single finger. "That you did, my dear." James leaned in, whispering into her ear. "Message received. I'll figure out a time to see you." His breath was warm against her neck, sending goosebumps down her back.

Throat dry, Rachel gulped. "I can't wait."

James nodded, kissing her quickly on the lips. "Go, or you'll be late." He released his embrace.

Untangling herself from his arms, Rachel reluctantly dragged her feet. "Until then." She forced herself to leave.

Lost in thought, Rachel walked the few blocks to the hospital. She wondered if this was what people felt when they were falling in love. It was fast and fierce. Of course, there had been others, others she believed she loved. But this was different, equal parts exhilarating and terrifying. In the middle of her racing thoughts, her phone rang.

Rachel dug her phone out of her purse, and after a quick glance at the screen, she answered, "Hello, Haley." Her voice was a tad too high.

"Tell me you saw him again," Haley sputtered. "I need to know."

Last night, after Rachel had returned home from her date with James, she had immediately called Haley and given her a full update on their budding romance. Haley was thrilled and reminded her she had known all along the two of them belonged together.

"It's good to hear from you too." Rachel chuckled.

"Yeah, yeah, I hear you," Haley said sarcastically. "Now give me the scoop."

Rachel quickly gave her an update on her morning interaction with James.

"I knew it." Haley wistfully sighed. "I'm always right about these things. Isn't that true?"

"Of course. How could I ever doubt you?" Rachel arrived at

the hospital. She switched her phone from one ear to the other. "I'm at work. I need to go."

"AHH, snap," Haley whined. "I take care of a baby all day. You're currently my only source of entertainment."

Rachel laughed. "I'm glad you find my love life entertaining. I'll call you after my shift."

"You better," Haley countered.

Rachel ended the call, entering the hospital lobby. Though Rachel had a twelve-hour shift, she couldn't help smiling. James was in her life, and her future was loaded with possibility.

CHAPTER FIFTEEN

Body aching, eyes heavy, James glanced at the time on the bottom of his laptop screen. He hadn't slept since before his date with Rachel yesterday. The darkness of night crept in as the city lights began to twinkle on the streets below. A bed had never sounded so good. He was dragging, big time. This contract was a nightmare. If he never saw it again, he'd be as happy as a clam. Standing, he stretched, trying to shake the stiffness in his neck and shoulders. The familiar pinch between his shoulder blades reminded him of the stresses of his deal.

The phone rang. Still standing, he grabbed his office phone off the hook. "Hello. This is James Ripley."

"James," his boss, Robert, replied. "I received the changes to the contract. I think this is going to work. I'll send it to the other side. We shouldn't have to respond till morning."

James slumped into his desk chair. The heavy weight of impending doom immediately lifted. "That's terrific news." He rested his elbows on his desk, running a hand down his face. Sighing, he said, "I'm relieved."

"Sorry, I was so brash with you yesterday." Robert cleared his throat. "I knew you would fix this whole thing, and you did. I apologize."

An apology from Robert—he'd take it. "No problem. This deal has all of us on edge. I promised to fix it, and I did." James yawned.

"I heard that. How long have you been up?" asked Robert.

Fading fast, James was practically lethargic. "Over thirty-six hours. My longest overnighter to date."

"A true badge of honor for those of us in big law," Robert said. "Go home and rest. You certainly earned it. See you tomorrow morning back at the office."

James bid goodbye and hung up the phone.

All he wanted to do was curl up on the couch in his office and sleep till morning. But he reeked and needed a shower badly. Quickly, he gathered up his things, flipping off the light. Naturally, on a late Sunday night, the office was eerily vacant and silent.

He strode across the darkened corridor and entered the elevator, which went down eighty floors in under two minutes. Making the fast descent, James grabbed his cell phone out of his pocket. There was a missed call from his friend Ryan. He texted him back, apologizing for being MIA. A lot had changed since their reunion several weeks back. Ryan responded, and they exchanged texts back and forth for the remainder of his elevator ride.

The elevator doors dinged then swooshed open. James spilled out into the lobby, making his way outside. Ryan's last text stared back at him on his phone screen.

Any new developments with Rachel?

James shook his head. Rachel. He promised he would text her, and the day had gotten completely away from him. Before he texted back to Ryan, he pulled up Rachel's number and messaged her.

> Thanks again for the breakfast burritos. I've been working for 30 hours. I'm finally heading home and plan on collapsing onto my bed.

Scrolling back to the text thread with Ryan, he typed rapidly.

> Oh yeah. So much to share, but I'm way too tired to explain it all right now. Let's meet up later this week.

Ryan instantly replied with a mind blown emoji followed with a GIF of Tom Cruise saying *You're the man.* James laughed and scrolled back to Rachel's name. She hadn't replied, so he slid his phone back into his pocket, walking the several blocks to the subway in a haze. Once home, he proceeded to curl up on his bed. He didn't even remove his clothes, but fell sound asleep within seconds.

Rachel knocked lightly on the patient's door. Once she heard the standard, "Come in," she opened the door and entered.

"Good evening. How are you doing? I'm Rachel and I'll be your nurse . . ." Her voice trailed off as she eyed the clock on the wall. "For the next four hours."

"I'm not good . . . not good." The woman twisted and grimaced in her bed. A monitor tracked her contractions. As the next wave began to appear on the monitor, she gripped the bed railing with one hand and her stomach with the other. "I . . . can't . . ." Her words came out in spurts. "Do . . . this."

Rachel went and washed her hands, then put on rubber gloves. The contraction ended, and Rachel approached her bedside. "Yes, you can." She glanced at the whiteboard to the side of the patient's bed. It listed all the patient's information in bold lettering, like name, support person, doctor, etc. "Miley, it's going to be okay."

With wild eyes, her nostrils flared. "How would you know?" Miley shrieked.

"Because I do this all day, every day. Plus, my favorite doctor is working tonight, Dr. Grayson. You're in good, capable hands." Rachel did a double take of the monitor, hoping she was seeing the vitals incorrectly. She wasn't. The baby's heart rate was low and almost into the danger zone. Adrenaline pumped through her veins. This wasn't good. She gnawed on her bottom lip. "When did the previous nurse check on you?"

"I'm not sure," Miley answered with closed eyes. She was taking deep breaths. "Maybe thirty minutes ago."

Rachel hit the call button, then used the phone on the bedstand to make a quick call to the nurses' station to page Dr. Grayson, but nobody answered. She hung up.

"Are you here all alone?" Rachel attempted to keep her voice steady, though her heart thundered.

"Yes." Miley twisted and turned in the hospital bed. "My husband is on a business trip, and my family lives out of state. I called him on my way to the hospital. He's trying to get here as fast as possible, but it's going to be a while. I have accepted I'll be giving birth alone. I didn't think I'd go into labor three weeks early." Sweat slathered her brow.

Rachel bit the inside of her cheek. Her gut told her this wasn't ending well. Pushing the thought away, she sprang into action, hoping against hope she was assessing the situation wrong.

"The baby is in a bit of distress." Rachel jogged to the doorway, glancing both ways to look for someone to alert Dr. Grayson, or any doctor for that matter.

Ellie passed by, but she halted in her tracks when she met Rachel's eyes.

"Ellie, page Dr. Grayson. I've tried, but he isn't answering. If he doesn't answer, I need another doctor in here STAT. The baby has bradycardia."

Her eyes widened. "I'm on it!" Ellie yelled over her shoulder as she dead-sprinted down the corridor of the hospital.

Rachel pivoted and strode back to Miley's bedside.

Miley sat straight up. "What's going on? Is my baby going to be okay?" She gripped her stomach as another contraction came. She cried out in pain. "TELL ME WHAT'S HAPPENING." The contraction wave subsided.

Peering over her shoulder toward the exit, Rachel prayed a doctor would enter soon. Her medical training could only take her this far without additional help. Nobody was in sight. She peered back at the monitor. Eyes glued to it; she patted the top of Miley's hand. "The baby's heart rate is dropping . . ." Her voice faded off.

Out of breath, Dr. Grayson came charging through the door-way. "Rachel, give me an update." He landed in front of the monitor, scanning the last few minutes of recorded information.

Rachel met Dr. Grayson's eyes. "The baby's heart rate has been dropping for the last few minutes. It's been hovering around 108 beats per minute for about two minutes."

Dr. Grayson nodded. "Okay. She's going in for an emergency C-section."

In unison, Rachel and Dr. Grayson unlocked the hospital bed wheels. They pushed Miley out of the delivery room down the hallway toward the operating room.

"What?!" Miley shrieked. The bed heaved forward, forcing Miley to lay her head back against the pillow. "My husband isn't even here . . . what if something bad happens?" She stared at Rachel, waiting for her to answer.

Rachel remained quiet. From previous years of experience, she knew in this situation it was best not to promise anything. Sometimes bringing a child into the world was risky business, and sometimes you lost the baby or the mother, or both. It was rare, but it did happen. Her mind reeled with the possible ending scenarios.

When neither Dr. Grayson nor Rachel responded, Miley patted the top of the bed, locating her cell phone. Her fingers slid across the screen, typing furiously into the phone. After she hit send, she attempted to call her husband. No response. They pushed her all the way into the operating room.

"I'll take it from here." Dr. Grayson peered over at Rachel as the surgery team took their positions.

Her middle recoiled. Both knew the outcome as the baby's heartbeat dropped even lower. She nodded. Pivoting, she walked back through the operating room doors in a daze. The blinding fluorescent lights made her temples throb as she strode back to the nurse's station.

Ellie glanced up from her computer screen when she arrived. "Any update?"

"Dr. Grayson is doing the emergency C-section right now." With shaky hands, she gripped the top of the nurses' station, leaning forward. "I think it was too late. The baby's heart rate was at 101."

Ellie stood, moving toward her. "You did everything you could." She held her arms out for an embrace. "Only time will tell."

Rachel hugged her back. "I know. I know." She broke their embrace, holding back the emotions wanting to surface. Pinching the bridge of her nose, she took a few settling breaths. Three more hours to go. Once her emotions were in check, Rachel continued, "I'd better do my rounds. I'm sure my other patients need my help. I've haven't been able to check on them at all in the last thirty minutes."

"Your patient in room twelve delivered with Dr. Teller." Ellie sat back down and continued typing. "The patient was moved up to the recovery floor."

Ellie and Rachel had worked together long enough to know,

in situations like these, you had to carry on until you heard an update. Rachel was forced to keep working.

"Thanks." Rachel pivoted, walking back toward the rooms of her other patients.

The final hours of her shift passed in a blur. In the mad dash between patient rooms, Rachel didn't have time to dwell on Miley. As her shift ended, she mulled over whether she should just clock out without finding out more. Ignorance was bliss, right? But her gut was eating itself, and Rachel knew she wasn't leaving until she had an update.

Rounding the corner, she went in search of Dr. Grayson. Soon, she spotted Dr. Grayson leaving a patient's room. With him in sight, a brick formed in her gut.

Rachel stopped in front of him in the hallway. "I'm off, but I needed to know how Miley is doing. Did the baby make it?" Her jaw tensed.

Hesitating, Dr. Grayson shook his head. "Unfortunately, no." Their eyes met as his brows furrowed. "Miley made it. I did everything I could to save the baby . . ." His voice trailed off, and he ran a hand down the length of his face.

He appeared devastated.

"I know you did," Rachel offered as a weak attempt to provide a little bit of comfort. "Did her husband make it here yet?"

"No, but he's on his way. He should be here in an hour or so." Dr. Grayson gave a small, almost undiscernible shrug. "I wish the outcome had been different, but sometimes these things are in God's hands, and there is absolutely nothing we can do about it."

"I know. That's where the faith part comes in." Rachel swiped at her misty eyes. "Believing there is someone who knows better than us. But no matter what, it's still always hard when we lose one."

"Agreed." Dr. Grayson wrung his hands. "I need to go. Have a nice night, Rachel."

Rachel said goodbye, and both walked in opposite directions.

Once in the locker room, she slumped onto the wooden bench. In the solitude of the empty room, Rachel allowed herself to cry. It was the one ugly part of her job, losing a patient. Once her emotions were in check, she opened the locker, retrieving her purse.

Leaving the locker room, Rachel told herself to head to the elevators. Her shift was over, and nobody would fault her in going straight home. Her feet ached and her body screamed for a hot shower to loosen the knots in her shoulders. But instead of taking the elevator, she pivoted and headed back to Miley's room.

Rachel only planned on taking a quick peek. Maybe her husband had finally arrived. If Miley had someone with her, then Rachel would be free to go home without saying anything. When she glanced through the little glass window on the door, she saw Miley all alone, sobbing.

Immediately, the tiredness and length of the day evaporated. Knocking lightly on the door, Miley gazed over at the door. They locked their eyes through the little window. Swiping at her face, Miley motioned for her to come in. Rachel entered.

"I'm so sorry." Rachel wiped her sweaty palms on the sides of her pants. She wished she were more eloquent. Wished she had a better way to convey the sincerity of her simple words. Wished things had turned out differently. Wished she was ending her shift to stop by and see a happy Miley, with a brand-new baby in her arms. But that wasn't the situation. The reality was she was only a nurse. A nurse with nothing else to offer than a few words. "I heard from Dr. Grayson your baby didn't make it."

Miley nodded, rocking back and forth on the bed. "My baby died." She shook uncontrollably. Her face fell forward into her palmed eyes, and she wept.

Rachel inched closer to the hospital bed. "Can I stay with you until your husband gets here?" Slowly, she lowered herself onto the corner of Miley's hospital bed. "I heard he won't be here for another hour or so. I don't want you to be alone." Her lip quivered as she forced herself to hold back the emotion bubbling up inside of her.

Miley cried some more without responding. Rachel wondered if her presence was unwanted. Shifting, she moved to stand.

"No please, you . . . can . . . stay." The words sputtered out into between wailing, heart-wrenching cries. Her body shook with convulsions.

Rachel moved closer, slowly wrapping her arms around Miley. Miley grabbed on tight, crying on her shoulder. The two cried together, embracing one another until her husband arrived. For the most part, Rachel loved her job, but sometimes, days like today made her world tilt off course. Sometimes the world seemed too dark and dreary. And all became too much. The weight, the burden, seemed too hard to carry. So, she gave it to God and knew with His help, she would soldier on.

CHAPTER SIXTEEN

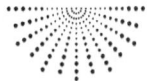

The morning sunshine peeked through James's curtains. He rolled to his side, stretching his arms high above his head. His mind was fuzzy. He wondered how long he had slept, because he couldn't remember the last time he felt this refreshed. Sitting up, he swung his legs over the side of the bed. Glancing at his bed stand, somehow, he managed to sleep for a solid eleven hours.

Swiping his cell phone off his bedstand, he checked the damage after his uninterrupted sleep. A few new emails, but nothing too urgent. The worst of things were behind him, and he breathed easier than he had in days. Rachel hadn't texted him back, so he shot her another text.

> I hope your shift went okay. I slept for a solid eleven hours. A new record.

Lingering for a few minutes, he waited for a response. When Rachel didn't send a reply, he left to shower and get ready for work.

Thirty minutes later, refreshed from his shower and food, he shoved his laptop into his bag. Though he'd arrive several hours later than usual, none of the other attorneys would mind. All knew the last few days for him had been torture. His cell phone pinged. The screen flashed a text message.

> Sorry I didn't respond to your earlier text. It was a long shift.

The three little cursor dots danced around at the bottom of the text message conversation. Rachel typed some more. He waited.

> One of my patients lost a baby in childbirth.

The words stared back at him. His stomach twisted round itself, twisting and turning the breakfast bagel he'd eaten minutes prior. Rachel worked with life and death as a labor and delivery nurse. A noble calling. While his work was long and arduous, it only involved money, not people's lives. Before she continued, he typed back.

> I'm sorry. Are you okay? Anything I can do?

Of course, Rachel wasn't okay. Immediately, James regretted his choice of words. Rachel was choosing to welcome him into her life, allowing him into the more intimate parts. James always had failed in this area of relationships. He had been alone for so long. James only knew how to carry the burdens of life by himself. But yesterday Rachel had buoyed up his spirit by bringing him breakfast. It was imperative he didn't push her away. James exited his apartment, riding the elevator down to the bottom floor.

His phone dinged once more. As he strode down the sidewalk, he pulled up her message.

> Thanks. Nothing for you to do. Somehow, I'll survive.

This was the moment. He knew it. His chance to do something out of the ordinary, provide comfort to the one he hoped would be his forever. James typed back.

> Are you home or back at work?

Halting in place, James leaned his back against the building he was passing by. While waiting for Rachel to respond, he tapped over to his work email, scanning through the latest emails that had come through. Nothing was pressing. If he arrived at his office by ten, nobody would question his absence. *Come on Rachel, tell me where you are so I can help you.*

His phone pinged.

> Home.

James hailed a taxi, giving the taxi driver the address of Rachel's apartment. The fare across Manhattan during rush hour would be astronomical, but he was a man on a mission. Rachel needed him. The feeling was exhilarating and freeing at the same time. It felt good to have someone to help.

Staring out the passenger window, James had no plan. When it came to wooing women, he struck out every time. What was he going to do to help Rachel? Then he remembered his friend Ryan. He always had a way with women. If anyone could help, it was Ryan. So, he pulled up his number on his phone and hit call.

The phone rang three times before Ryan picked up. "Hey, James," Ryan replied.

"Ryan," James sputtered out, then pressed forward. "I need your advice. I need to do something for Rachel. She had a bad day at work. Help me, man. I've got nothing."

Ryan cleared his throat. "Well . . ." His voice faded off. It sounded like he was talking to someone else in the room.

When the connection seemed like it had been lost, James

pulled his phone away from his ear, checking the screen. Then he brought it back to his ear. "You still with me, Ryan?" James ran his free hand through his hair.

"Yeah, I'm here." There was some rustling on his end. Ryan continued, "I'm putting you on speaker. I'm here with Chloe. She might be able to help. Women know more about these types of things."

"Chloe is in New York?" James spit out, nearly choking. "When did all of this happen?"

"It's been happening over the last few weeks," Ryan stated, followed by a long pause. "You've been MIA."

"You're right. I'm sorry." James wished he had been a better friend and made more of an effort to connect with him.

Chloe broke the silence. "James, I'm here. What do you need help with?"

A million questions flipped through his mind, but none landed. "How long are you in town, Chloe?" asked James.

Chloe chuckled. "Forever. I moved here for good last week."

James opened his mouth to speak but thought better of it. Backpedaling through his first thoughts, he finally stated, "I think you two are great together. I'm happy for the both of you."

"Thanks," Ryan answered. "Now, enough about how great we look together. We already know that."

Chloe laughed. "Tell us how we can help."

The taxi changed lanes, causing him to slam against the window. He gripped onto the armrest. Quickly, he explained his dates with Rachel, their budding romance, and his most recent text exchange.

Chloe answered, "James, I really don't think you can go wrong with picking up some food and drinks for her like she did for you."

James shook his head. Surely, the answer couldn't be so simple. "That's it?"

"Yes." Chloe let out an exasperated sigh. "It really is that easy. I don't get why guys don't get that. If you simply make a little bit of effort, doing a small act to show you care goes miles for us."

"Do you know any of her favorite foods?" asked Ryan.

"No." He wished he had asked.

Besides Thai food, and her love of breakfast burritos, James didn't know any more. Man, he had a long way to go to have a fully functional relationship.

"Where does she live?" asked Chloe.

"East Village."

The taxi stopped at a light.

"There's a great breakfast place that has stuffed French toast. I fell in love with the place last time I visited. Get her that. I'll text you the info right now," stated Chloe.

"I'd appreciate it." The taxi came to a halt in front of Rachel's apartment building. James adjusted his bag on his shoulder and paid the taxi driver before he exited. "I need to go. I'm here."

"Good luck buddy," added Ryan.

"Thanks. And again, I'm happy for both of you." James lingered in front of Rachel's apartment. "Let's all meet up again soon."

James ended the call. Seconds later, his phone pinged with the address of the breakfast place Chloe suggested. He was in luck; it was right around the corner.

Twenty minutes later, with food in hand, James stared up at Rachel's apartment building. Juggling the bag of food and his shoulder bag, James knew he wouldn't even have time to eat with her. A ten o'clock call was scheduled while he waited for the food.

After he climbed the stairs and regained his breath, James knocked lightly on the door. Within seconds, it swung open, and Rachel's roommate, Amber, stared back at him with narrowed eyes. "It's you again." Her voice was laced with hatred.

James shook the bag of food. "Yes. I brought Rachel breakfast."

"Well." Amber rolled her eyes, crossing her arms. "Aren't you just a knight in shining armor?" Under her breath, she muttered, "Give me a break."

He chose to ignore her cynicism and instead dug into the to-go bag and fished out the extra meal he planned on keeping for himself. "I brought an extra meal for you, too. Do you like French toast?" asked James.

The permanent scowl on her face lessened a tad. Her lips almost formed a small smile. "It happens to be my favorite." Her voice was devoid of enthusiasm.

"Here." James pushed the to-go box into her hands. "It's yours. I'm glad it's your favorite. I'll certainly remember that for the future." He peered past Amber, glancing into the small apartment, hoping to see a sign of Rachel. "Is Rachel home?"

Amber slightly opened the to-go box, peeking inside. The smell of cinnamon and eggs eked out, making James's stomach rumble, though he'd had a bagel earlier. He regretted not purchasing three meals, but if he managed to win over Amber and make Rachel's living situation less hostile, then a hungry morning was the least he could sacrifice.

"She's home." Amber pushed the door all the way open, allowing space for James to enter. "I'll go let her know you're here." She disappeared down the narrow hallway.

A few moments later, Amber returned, with Rachel trailing along behind her. Rachel appeared in baggie sweatpants and an oversized open sweater. Her hair was thrown up in a messy bun. She pulled the front of her sweater tighter around her middle, holding it closed. With her other hand, she attempted to tuck some loose strands of hair behind her ears.

A small smile grew across her face. "James." Rachel tilted her head to the side. "This is a nice surprise. What are you doing here?"

James held up the to-go bag. "I brought you breakfast. You had a hard day, and I wanted to cheer you up. You made yesterday better for me, and I wanted to do the same for you in return."

Amber sat down at the two-top table a few steps away from them. She opened the to-go box and began to eat, studying them closely but remaining silent.

Rachel's face lit up. "Thanks." She stepped closer, and James handed Rachel the bag of food. Rachel took it from him, glancing down at the bag. "Thank you. This was very thoughtful of you."

James shrugged. "It was nothing. I wish I could stay, but I need to be at work for a call in twenty minutes." He shuffled his feet, double-checking his watch.

Rachel furrowed her brow. "Oh, okay."

It made him square his shoulders. Maybe she did care about him as much as he cared about her?

"I'm sorry." James ran a hand down the length of her arm, memorizing it. "You know I'd spend the whole day with you if I could."

Meekly, Rachel smiled. "I wish you didn't have to run off, but I appreciate you stopping by and bringing food. It is my love language after all."

"Oh." James smirked. "I remember."

"I like this one," Amber interrupted.

Both shifted, peering over at her. James had completely forgotten Amber was even there.

Amber chewed, then swallowed, shaking her fork at him. "This guy is way better than the last jerk you dated."

"Thanks." Rachel crinkled her nose. Then she shifted back, re-centering her focus on him. She winked. "I think so too."

The words made warmth pool in his middle, while his heart rate tripled its speed. This woman had him hook, line and sinker, and he welcomed it. Without missing a beat, Rachel leaned in, kissing him lightly on the lips. She pulled away, giving his shoulder a squeeze.

"Thanks for coming." Rachel's cheeks tinted pink.

Mind muddled, James stumbled a few steps backwards, nearly tripping over the threshold. Regaining his balance, he grabbed onto the door frame. *Nobody ever said you were smooth.*

"Text or call me if you need anything." He swiveled and headed out of the apartment. Over his shoulder he said, "I mean it. I want to be here for you."

Rachel took a step out of the apartment and into the hallway. "I will." She wrung her hands together. "I would like to do the same for you, too."

James said goodbye and made his exit, taking the stairs two at a time. He didn't even mind the steady stream of sweat dripping down his back. By the time he reached outside, his clothes were stuck to his skin. None of it mattered, and he hardly noticed the overly hot and muggy air. His phone went haywire in his pocket, beeping and buzzing with emails, calls, and messages. He waited for the stress to settle in, but it didn't. James was a man in love. And this time she might even at least like him back.

Rachel went back into her apartment.

Amber glanced up mid-bite. "You'd be a fool to let that one go." She took another bite of the French toast, almost smiling, which was practically a minor miracle. It looked like James had a way of winning women over, Amber included.

"I know." Rachel grabbed the other to-go box out of the bag, settling down at the table across from Amber. "He's certainly the nicest guy I've ever dated."

"And HOT. Don't forget about that part." Amber raised an eyebrow, locking eyes with her. "It never hurts the ego to have a man like him be interested in you."

Rachel laughed. "He is easy on the eyes, isn't he?" She opened the to-go box and doused her French toast with syrup before she took a bite. "Mm." Rachel smacked her lips together. "This is delicious."

"I told you." Amber continued to eat. "You might have met your person."

Due to Amber's brash personality, and Rachel's busy work schedule, the roommates spent very little time together. But James managed to butter Amber up with free food, and Rachel planned on taking full advantage of the opportunity to improve their relationship.

Casually, Rachel asked, "Are you dating anyone?" She cut another piece of the French toast.

Amber scoffed. "Me, date?" With a wave of her hand, she continued, "Not a chance. I've had too many bad experiences. One too many times of getting my hopes up, only to have them dashed. I don't know if or when I'll ever be ready to travel down that road again." Her face was devoid of emotion, more simply resolved.

Rachel wholeheartedly understood her level of frustration. It was a long and arduous process to find someone you clicked with on the necessary levels. Then, when you had nobody in your life, it always seems like everyone else around you was in love. Nobody ever said dating was easy.

"I hear you." Rachel met her glance, letting compassion seep into her voice. "I've had very similar experiences."

"I don't believe that for a minute." Amber tilted her face to the side. "You're so put together. Everything seems to go your way."

"I'm flattered I've fooled you. But my life is far from put together. If anything, I'm the exact opposite. My life has been one long string of bad relationships. I partly work so much because it's the one place I feel in control," replied Rachel.

At least work used to be a place where she felt confident. After her last delivery, she was rattled, and part of her was questioning her skill and ability. The long list of doubts came creeping in, and she had to remind herself sometimes deliveries ended tragically. Sometimes things couldn't be prevented. Even with this reasoning, Rachel hoped she could move past yesterday and continue to find joy and fulfillment in being a nurse.

"I can understand that." Amber closed her empty to-go box and stood. "I need to get back to work." She tossed the box into the trash. "It was nice talking to you, Rachel."

Rachel glanced up at her. "Same." She smiled.

Amber left, wandering back to her bedroom. Rachel finished eating. After all the trash was put away, she shot James a text message.

> Best French toast ever. Thanks again.

Stalling in the kitchen for James to reply, Rachel wiped off the counter and table. Her phone pinged. She swiped it off the table, bringing up his text.

> I'm glad. I hope you feel better. I'll call you tonight.

Rachel smiled. Maybe with James in her life, she would discover her equilibrium once again.

CHAPTER SEVENTEEN

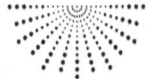

The next several weeks passed quickly, and Rachel reveled in her whirlwind romance.

Days were filled with exchanges of text messages and phone calls. Somehow, with both of their hectic schedules, they managed to sneak in dates. Every possible minute available to her, Rachel wanted to spend with James. This surely was what she had been waiting for her entire life.

Late one night, Rachel strode with James through Central Park. All the trees lining the path had changed from crisp green to the brilliant colors of fall: yellow, orange, and red. She gazed up at the long branches smattered with their variety of color, admiring the beauty in her surroundings.

"James, don't you love New York in the fall?" Rachel breathed in the luscious smell. Gratitude and happiness seeped into her entire being.

James gave her hand a squeeze, his eyes finding hers, sending a shiver down her spine. "I believe it's the best season by far. Summer is too hot, winter is too cold, and spring is too rainy."

Rachel smiled, stopping in her tracks. "See, you totally get me." She leaned in and lightly kissed him.

Brushing a few loose strands of her hair behind her ear, James brought an arm around her waist, drawing their bodies closer. "I like to think so," he whispered.

"You do." Rachel took in the entire hunky image of him, making her face flush. "You really see me, and you accept me as I am. I appreciate it. I've never had that before—with anyone."

"You're the perfect one for me." James kissed her lightly on the temple. "I've liked you for as long as I can remember . . ." His voice trailed off, and he peered up the sidewalk in front of them.

James had many memories of her over the years. She, on the other hand, had very few. Only a few hazy passing moments in high school. Every now and then, James revealed another one of his hidden memories—moments which meant a lot to him—and it made her regret that she hadn't seen him back then. Not in the way she saw him now.

Rachel stood on her tiptoes, leaning into him, and kissed him. "I wish I remembered you from back then, but I'm happy you're in my life now."

"You . . . being with you . . ." James brought her closer to him. She rested a hand on his chest. His hand dove into her hair, cradling the back of her neck. His eyes skidded across her face, making her feel beautiful. "It means everything."

The moment of intensity was palpable. She stumbled over how to respond. "Ditto."

James boldly held her gaze. He gulped.

"I love you."

The words dangled in the air between them, dipping and diving, then finally landing in the middle of her heart. She moved her hand from his chest to his face, cupping his cheek. "I think I love you too."

His eyes dilated. "You do?" His voice cracked.

"Don't act so surprised." Playfully, Rachel hit him on the arm. "You know I do."

James grabbed her by the waist, lifting her off the ground.

"Woohoo!" he shouted. Vibrant and alive, his voice traveled down the pathway through the upcoming tunnel.

He spun her around in a circle while Rachel giggled. When her feet touched the ground again, she tugged him closer, letting her lips skim across his. James tightened his grip around her waist, bringing their bodies closer. He twisted his fingers into her hair while his thumbs stroked the slope of her jaw.

Rachel couldn't remember a time when she felt this beautiful, this loved. Here, kissing James, the stresses of the day dissipated, along with the worries of the future and what any of this meant.

As the wind picked up, her hair fluttered this way and that, whipping his tangy aftershave along with it. Her nostrils flared, making her dizzy. How long they remained there, embracing, kissing, Rachel had no clue. Because she wanted to live there in that beautiful moment of lovely, perfect bliss forever. James made her world sparkly and special, and she wanted to believe this relationship would go the distance.

Heart nearly exploding, she forced her lips away from his. Rachel snuggled her head against his chest as she waited for her breathing to return to normal. James stroked her hair in long, even movements. Eventually, Rachel pulled away.

James wrapped his arm around her shoulders. Rachel mirrored his movement, placing her arm around his waist. The two exited Central Park, walking toward Rachel's apartment. Even when the loud sounds of the city became clear once more, she only heard the steady thump of her heart. This was her chance at happiness, and she was taking it. Nothing was going to derail her love for him. Because she naively believed love could conquer all.

CHAPTER EIGHTEEN

A month later, James was at work. Deep in thought, he flinched when Robert appeared in the doorway of his office and said, "Do you think the deal will close this Friday as planned?"

Shifting in his seat, James shuffled the documents scattered across his desk. When he found the correct ones, he finally responded, "I don't know . . ." His voice trailed off. He moved his gaze from Robert back to the documents. He wasn't overly familiar with the case, but was being pulled in on it at the last minute to help out Robert. Immediately, James spotted various problems that would take more than a few days to fix. He looked back up, paused, then finally said, "It's doubtful. There are too many problems with this draft. You need to ask for more time."

Robert brought his hand into a fist and tapped it against the doorway. "This can't be happening," he groaned. "You don't think there's a slight possibility it could happen by then?"

"No. It's impossible." His jaw clenched, and James tried his best to sound calm and collected.

Robert groaned louder.

In the past, James probably would have worked around the

clock to take on any project or task which needed his help. Not this time. Things were different. He had Rachel. Robert needed to accept sometimes things simply weren't possible and deadlines needed to be renegotiated. Even though James still had every intention of being a good and dutiful attorney, he also needed to have a sliver of self-preservation. He decided to take a stand.

"Ask for an extra week," James continued. "The other side sat on this for a month, and I don't see why they're demanding we return the changes in such a short amount of time." He leaned back in his chair, raising his hands to cup the back of his neck. "That's their fault, not ours."

"I—" Robert shoved his hands into his pockets. He closed his eyes for a moment before he continued, "I'll ask for an extra week. If the two of us work on this together, would it be manageable to finish it by the new deadline?" He raised an eyebrow.

Shifting forward, James rested his elbows on his desk. "I believe it can be done. The previous date is a total joke."

Usually, Robert pushed back, demanding James needed to drop everything. But he remained eerily rational. Maybe James's newly imposed boundaries with work might pay off.

"Okay," Robert grumbled. "Hopefully you don't have plans for this weekend."

James exhaled. "I suppose I no longer do."

He wanted to argue, shake his fist at the injustice of it all, but his job required him to be at the mercy of the client. He'd miss out on spending the weekend with Rachel. Unfortunately, this wasn't the first time he had canceled plans with her due to work. Hopefully, canceling again wouldn't create problems between them. The last thing he wanted was for Rachel to question if she was the most important thing in the world to him.

"Thanks. I knew I could count on you." Robert pivoted to leave. "I'll email you about the necessary changes." Then he left.

The whole situation was far from ideal, but at least the new deadline wasn't soul crushing. He went back to work, making necessary changes to the agreement. The morning hours sped by. It wasn't until he heard the sound of his cell phone ringing that he broke from the trance. Swiping his phone off the top of his desk, he checked the number.

A smile spread across his face. He clicked accept, placing it to his ear. "Rachel. Just the one I was thinking about." He stretched his stiff neck back and forth.

"James," Her voice cracked. The sound was muffled. "I . . ." Her voice trailed off again, and she sniffled.

Sitting straight up in his chair, James responded, "Rachel, is everything okay? What's going on?"

"No, everything isn't okay," Rachel wailed.

James's stomach plummeted, while his mind ran wild with the possibility of worst-case scenarios. He ran his fingers through his hair, then down the length of his face. "What happened?" He managed to sputter out.

"It's—my—" Her voice shook. "My dad had a stroke. I need to go home and be with my mom. I don't know how bad it is, but . . ."

A stroke. James hoped it wasn't serious. Of course, she needed to go to Cloverton to be with her family. Cloverton. The mere thought of that town made his stomach sour and palms sweat. *It's okay. She'll go. You'll stay. And then she'll come back.* That's if her dad made a quick recovery. A tight knot took up residence between his shoulder blades.

"It'll be okay." James rubbed the back of his neck. The words fell flat even to his own ears. Who knew if her dad would ever recover? But the truth was, he had no idea what else to say. His experience with family was slim. *Avoid at all costs* had been his motto. Though it was a thousand steps ahead, he hoped someday her family would be his too. "When are you leaving?"

"I booked a flight out of JFK." The shakiness in her voice

evened out as Rachel continued, "I should be there by evening. I wish you could come with me. Please come with me."

Come with her? To Cloverton? James inwardly groaned.

A long pause followed. It made his skin crawl. The doubt began to creep in. The reality being their new relationship might not be strong enough to face this type of storm. What if Rachel never came back? What if she decided her parents needed her there permanently? James shook the feeling of the shaky future away and bottled the doubt back up.

"Rachel," James spoke up.

"Yeah." Rachel sighed, making him wish he was different. Making him wish he was whole.

"I love you. I wish I could be there with you, but I'm in the middle of a big case." James cringed.

A case? It sounded like a poor excuse, even to himself. Who knew what would happen to her dad? Rachel would think he was choosing work over her. If only he had the ability to explain everything, to let her know he wanted more than anything to be her support person, but James had too much going on right now. All his deadlines spun around in his head, making his judgement impaired.

James heard Rachel exhale sharply.

Major mistake. He still had time to backtrack, to figure out some way to make it work.

But like an idiot, James continued, "I can't go with you." He wiped at the sweat slick across his brow.

"It's always work . . ." Rachel's voice trailed off. The words gutted him, but he didn't correct her. "I'll talk to you later." She hung up without saying I love you or goodbye.

James tossed the phone on top of his desk. Leaning forward, he gathered his face into his flat-palmed hands. A sinking feeling overcame him. This was the end. He knew it. And it was all his fault.

With jittery hands, Rachel ended her call with James. Over the past few months of dating, his work had been the black cloud hanging over them. At first Rachel understood, she too worked long hours, picking up extra shifts whenever possible, but James's work always came first to *everything*. Even to her. She tried to be understanding, to not make a mountain out of a molehill, but her patience was wearing thin. The one time she asked for him to pick her first and support her, he refused.

Could this be a red flag? One she had overlooked? The first inkling of doubt encroached into her mind. This might be a deal breaker. Shaking off the entire interaction, Rachel instead chose to spring into action.

Frantically, she threw a hodgepodge of items into her suitcase. Only a few minutes earlier, when her mom had called from the hospital with the news, she promised herself she wouldn't panic. Not now, not when she didn't know what the future held. A stroke had a broad spectrum of outcomes, and Rachel hoped her dad would make a full recovery. Instead, she needed to focus on getting to Cloverton. If she didn't, Rachel would fall apart.

Luckily her brother, Daniel, lived in Cloverton with his new wife, Ashley. Daniel and Ashley worked as teachers at the local high school and were on the way to the hospital to be with her mom. It gave Rachel comfort to know her mom wouldn't be alone. What if her dad ended up—nope, she wasn't traveling down that road. Anxiety pulsed through her veins while she gave the room a final glance.

Barreling out of her bedroom, Amber, who was on the couch, glanced up from her laptop. "Everything okay?" She raised an eyebrow while sitting straight up.

"No." Rachel popped into the bathroom, grabbing random toiletries. She tossed them into her bag, hoping they were the correct sizes for a carry-on. If not, she would throw them away and buy what she needed in Cloverton.

In the midst of her frantic search in the bathroom, Amber appeared in the doorway, watching Rachel maneuver around it, looking for items. "What's going on? Anything I can do to help?" She crossed her arms, leaning against the door frame.

Tears tickled the corner of her eyes, and Rachel blinked rapidly to keep them at bay. "My dad had a stroke." Her voice cracked, and she averted her eyes. "I need to go home."

"I'm so sorry." Amber shifted, her voice laced with compassion as she sought Rachel's eye. "I hope he ends up being okay. Is there anything I can do to help?"

Eyes stinging, Rachel took a deep breath and pinched the bridge of her nose. The dam was about to break, and she didn't have time to deal with it. She needed to get to JFK pronto.

"Umm." Rachel regained her composure. "Sorry, I'm stressed I need to get to JFK within the next thirty minutes or I won't make my flight."

"Let me set up an Uber for you. My treat." Amber stepped back from the doorway into the hall, pulling out her phone from her pocket. Her finger flew across the screen.

"I can't let you do that." Rachel zipped her carry-on bag closed. "An Uber at rush hour will cost you a fortune."

Amber waved her off without looking up from her phone. "I want to help. This is the one thing I can do." She continued to swipe and type, then after one big tap, Amber slid her phone back into her back pocket. "All set. Uber will be here in five minutes. Plenty of time to make it to the airport on time."

Rachel reached out, pulling Amber in for a slightly awkward hug. "Thanks. I truly appreciate it. My mind's racing a mile a minute, and you just took something off my plate." She pulled away, grabbing her carry-on bag. Flipping off the bathroom light, Rachel wheeled her suitcase out to the living room. Amber trailed along behind her. "I guess I'd better go." She strode to the door and opened it. Pivoting, she glanced back at Amber. "I don't know when I'll be back."

"That's understandable," Amber stated, taking a step closer. "I'll be thinking about you. I guess I'll see you when I see you."

Adjusting her purse on her shoulder, Rachel nodded. Then she left, hoping it wasn't her last time in her apartment.

CHAPTER NINETEEN

Later that evening, long past when the others in the office had gone home, James worked with Robert furiously from the conference room table. Rachel must have landed, but she hadn't responded to any of his text messages. Not knowing if her dad was okay was eating him alive. He wanted to be there with her, to be the one to provide her comfort in her time of need, but he couldn't go. Traveling to see Rachel meant returning to Cloverton. His stomach recoiled at the idea of revisiting the hospital where his own mother had died, but even he knew sometimes you must do the difficult things to show someone you truly cared. And James didn't want Rachel to question his commitment to her.

Work was an excuse, and he knew it. If he was smart, he'd book a ticket and meet Rachel in Cloverton tonight. He'd throw caution to the wind and trust somehow everything would work out.

With his current contract, he wouldn't be freed up to go anywhere until next Friday. A whole ten days away. Ten days. He had gone ten *years* without seeing Rachel. Ten years of longing to see her in the flesh. And she had been everything he remembered and more. His life was better because Rachel was in it. If he lost her over this, James didn't think he could recover. The mere thought filled his heart with a dull ache, one he couldn't shake.

From the other side of the highly glossed wood conference table, Robert highlighted a portion of the agreement. A loud squeak sounded with each flick of his highlighter.

James shifted in his chair, glancing up at the clock. It was past midnight. "Robert, can I ask you something personal?"

Robert stopped mid-highlight and peered over at him. He cocked an eyebrow. "Umm, I guess." His voice was laced with apprehension.

"How have you managed to stay married all these years?" James leaned back in his chair, cradling the back of his neck with his hands. "I mean, you're one of the few at this firm who has remained married to the same woman for—how many years?"

"Thirty-three," Robert responded without hesitation. He put the cap back on his highlighter, tossing it onto the tabletop. "Honestly . . ." His voice trailed off while he looked out the wall of full-length windows overlooking the city. "I married the right woman."

James raised an eyebrow. "That's it?"

Surely, the answer couldn't be that easy. But how did he know he had found the right one? How did the struggles of life not end up pulling them apart? This event with Rachel's dad might be his relationship's demise.

Robert chuckled. "Yes. That's it." He stood, stretching his arms high above his head. "I'm not saying the thirty-three years hasn't had its challenges. As you know, this job is high stress, long hours, and an unpredictable schedule. I mean, the list goes on and on."

Robert sat back down. His demeanor was more relaxed than James had ever seen him. They rarely discussed personal matters, but one thing he did admire about Robert was his family. He had brought his family over the years to firm functions, and always spoke about them with pride.

"But," Robert continued, "my wife is my everything. When I met her... I just knew. I knew I would move heaven and earth for us to be together. And I still would. My wife does the same. With us both working together every day to make each other happy, everything else manages to click into place."

"No way." James shook his head. His voice was more cynical than he wanted. "It can't be that simple. I think you're lying to me."

He wondered if he even had the capability to give everything to someone else. To fully trust that the other person wanted what was best for him. His entire life, he had only trusted in himself. Everyone in his life, specifically his family, had let him down or left him out. Rachel might be the rare exception.

"It really is. Marriages usually go south when people let selfishness creep in. However, if you care about the other person's happiness as much as your own, then you'll be fine." Robert gave him a sideways glance. "Why? Are you thinking about getting married?"

Heat splashed his cheeks, and James shifted uncomfortably in his seat. "I don't think so. There's someone I love, but I don't know if it will work out." His voice faded off as his heart twinged with an ache.

He hoped things would work out with Rachel, but he was too much of a realist to believe they were already in the clear. If anything, their relationship was only beginning to face obstacles.

"How does your wife deal with your long hours?" countered James.

His hours were a hot button with Rachel. And had been with every other person he had dated.

Robert forced a laugh. "Not well." Then he waved a hand. "No, but really, it's something we've had to work through. She gives me a list of priorities. Things we have both agreed I need to be at, and then she manages to be understanding with all the other times I cancel last minute."

Rachel's situation certainly should take precedence over work. James knew he was in the wrong, especially because she asked him to come with her. The one time she asked for something important, he failed. His neck and shoulders ached. How was he this bad at relationships? Had he learned nothing from his past? Apparently, he hadn't.

When James didn't elaborate, Robert gave a curt nod, picking up his highlighter again. His pen squeaked across the paper.

"If you ever want to talk about it," Robert didn't look up, but kept his focus on his paper, "I'm here to listen."

"Thanks. I appreciate it." James went back to editing the document on his laptop. "I'll keep that in mind."

Thirty minutes later, a text came from Rachel.

> I made it to Cloverton. Things are worse than I thought.

> I'm sorry. How bad?

> He has paralysis on the left side of his body and impaired speech. It might be permanent.

Oh dear. I'm sorry. That's horrible news.

He's gone in for surgery. I'm still waiting to hear more.

James and Robert continued working mostly in silence until around 2 a.m., when they finally called it quits. Defeated and exhausted, James climbed into the back of his Uber. Scrolling through his last string of text messages with Rachel, he felt torn in different directions. He longed to be with Rachel, but yet James remained in NYC.

Cloverton. His chest pinched tight as James remembered his mom and the last few days of her life. A painful and confusing time in his life, but the years that followed were unbearable.

James knew the devastation that came from losing a parent. Leaning his cheek against the passenger window of the Uber, he allowed the cool glass to fight the fiery burn of his cheeks. He stared out at the city lights and quiet streets. Each block he passed, he became resolved he couldn't go to Cloverton tonight. James forced himself to type a quick response to Rachel's text.

> I'm only now heading home. I miss you already. I wish I could be there with you. I love you, Rachel.

He hit send, knowing full well his words weren't enough. Love was an action, and he questioned his ability to rise to the occasion.

A few minutes later, the Uber halted in front of his apartment building. He climbed out. His phone pinged while closing the car door.

> I'm still at the hospital. I wish you were here too. I could use the support. Good night, James.

Exhaling, James headed into his apartment. His relationship was at stake. He couldn't lose Rachel, he wouldn't survive. If he was smart, he would drop everything to be with her. James didn't like Cloverton, but for Rachel, he should be willing to do anything. Then James remembered his job and the deadlines he faced. Though his job shouldn't be more than important than his relationship, James's whole identity was wrapped up in being good at being an attorney. Being successful in his profession provided James with stability, direction, and pride. What was he going to do? A mangled mess, James made the wrong choice and simply went to bed.

Rachel paced the tiny waiting room, biting on her bottom lip so hard she tasted blood.

"Rachel, you need to sit down." Daniel, her brother, patted the seat next to him. "You're walking the carpet bare. Plus, it's making me nervous." His wife, Ashley, sat next to him, their fingers intertwined.

Sharon, her mom, sat across from them, wringing her hands together. When Rachel arrived, her dad had already gone into surgery. The doctors believed he had suffered a hemorrhagic stroke, and they were attempting to stop the bleeding in his brain without causing further damage.

Sharon reached out from where she sat, tugging her daughter's arm. "Sit down, Rachel." Her voice was more of a command than a suggestion. "The doctor said he should be out of surgery soon. Then we'll have a better idea of your dad's state."

Rachel wiggled her arm out of Sharon's grasp. "I know, Mom." She shook her arms at her side, trying to dampen the nerves pulsing through her veins. "I just can't sit still any longer. I feel like a caged animal in here."

Daniel unlocked his hand from Ashley's, wrapping his arm around Ashley's shoulders. He cleared his throat, paused, then stated, "Mom was telling us all about this guy, James." He half smirked. "Please, tell us more about him. It will keep all our minds off Dad for a minute."

Rachel narrowed her eyes at Sharon.

Sharon meekly smiled. "I only mentioned him in passing." She shrugged.

With a huff, Rachel flung herself into the chair next to her mom, sitting knee to knee, in the pint-size room, across from Ashley and Daniel.

"I can't believe Mom told you about him," Rachel groaned, crossing her arms protectively against herself. "We've only been dating a few months." She avoided eye contact with all of them by glancing out the window.

She hated telling her family about potential love interests, because she had traveled down this road too many times to count. Her family became too invested too soon in the guys she dated. When things ended, because they always did, they were more devastated than her. Everyone wanted her paired off, including herself, but the fact was, James wasn't here. Even when she asked him to come, he didn't. Nor did he show any sign of ever coming.

The rejection deflated her ego a smidge. If the situation had been reversed and it had been his family member, Rachel would've dropped everything to be with him. Apparently, things only ran one way. Maybe she had gotten swept away in the romance of the relationship. The fact he had always loved her—who didn't want to hear that? Perhaps naively, she had looked past the red flags. Any man who chose work over you, continually, might not be the one for you.

"Rachel, don't be mad," Ashley piped up. "All of us simply want you to find a nice guy." She forced a smile.

A pause followed. Rachel didn't comment but kept her gaze down at her feet. If they wanted to know more, they would have to pry it out of her.

Ashley leaned her elbow on the armrest, cradling her chin. "Come on Rachel, tell us about him. We heard you met him at your high school reunion. I mean, how cute is that?" She exchanged a goo-goo-eyed look with Daniel.

Rachel shook her head while catching the hint of mischievousness in the exchange between Daniel and Ashley.

"What happened with what's-his-bucket?" Daniel asked in a mocking tone. "The one you've been in love with since who knows when."

Through gritted teeth, Rachel replied, "Brandon."

As far as she was concerned, he was a distant memory she never wanted to revisit.

Daniel snapped, then pointed. "That's his name. *Brandon.* What a jerk. This other guy—" He glanced at her for help.

"James," Rachel exhaled, her shoulders drooping.

"Yes, James. He sounds way better. Mom says he's some hot-shot attorney." Daniel looked at her with pride. "I mean well done, Rachel. I'm impressed."

Ashley squeezed Daniel on the knee. "He sounds great."

Rachel rubbed her hands back and forth over her thighs. "Thanks. We'll see what the future holds for us. It's too soon to tell."

Rachel peered out the window to her side. The dark night sky made it impossible to see out, and instead she was confronted with her haggard appearance. Dark circles took up residence under her eyes, and her hair was haphazardly thrown into a messy, unkempt bun. All this talk of James made her wonder about their entire relationship.

After an eternity, Rachel finally commented, "He is a 'hot-shot' attorney, and because of it, he works long and unpredictable hours. He might not have space in his life for me, or, frankly, for anyone."

James. James. James. She wanted him here with her. She missed him. Perhaps the seriousness of the situation brought new light to their relationship. Maybe James wasn't ready for the heavy stuff. Maybe it was all for the best. Time for her to get out before it became too hard to walk away.

"I'm sure if you two really care about each other, you'll find a way to make it work." Sharon offered.

"That's a nice thought, Mom." Rachel's lips formed a tight, straight line. "But sometimes it's not enough. Sometimes, time and distance wreak havoc and have their way with a relationship working out. No matter how good the initial connection might be, sometimes nothing can prevent it from crashing and burning." With a jutted chin, she gave her a pointed look.

"Don't be," Sharon slapped her lightly on her arm, "such a Debbie Downer." She tsked.

"Yeah, sis, don't be such a cynic," said Daniel with a smirk.

Rachel threw her hands up. "Says a man who's already *married.*" She raised an eyebrow.

Daniel squirmed uncomfortably in his seat. The two of them had an unwritten rule to not meddle in each other's love lives. Rachel had never given him grief over the years about all the various women he had dated until he found Ashley. His conquests had been numerous.

"Enough, you two," stated Sharon. "I can see Rachel doesn't want to talk about this mystery guy. I'll drop it."

With a smile, Rachel replied, "Great. Fine by me." She crossed her arms and stared out the window.

The rest of the time passed slowly. Whenever a doctor or nurse shuffled by, all turned to see if one of them was coming to deliver news about her dad's status. Finally, a doctor approached them.

Sharon stood, wringing her hands. "Do you have an update for us?" Her voice was laced with anxiety.

Rachel stood too, wrapping her arm around her mom's shoulders, hoping to provide her with some needed support.

"Yes. I'm Dr. Cromwell. We were able to stop the bleeding in his brain, but we won't know how much damage the stroke caused to Eric's speech and movement for a few more days." Dr. Cromwell flipped through the paperwork in his hands, reading a few of the sections. Eventually, he stopped and peered up at them. "In addition, unfortunately, he most likely has permanent paralysis on the left side of his body. Again, you'll have to be patient. We'll know more over the next few days."

Rachel swallowed down the bile creeping up her throat. Her heart plummeted. Up until this moment, Sharon had been remarkably stoic, but this crushed her. Gripping Rachel's shoulder tightly, Sharon rested her head on her daughter and wailed. Ashley came closer to Sharon, rubbing her back in long, hypnotic strokes while she cried.

"We'll figure it all out," said Ashley, barely above a whisper. She peered over at Daniel, who stood at her side in a daze. Daniel didn't speak up, but instead pushed his hands into his pockets, speechless. Ashley turned back to Sharon and continued, "You have us to help you."

Daniel's face was devoid of emotion. Robotically, he pulled his hand out of his pocket and held it out to a lingering Dr. Cromwell. "We appreciate the update. Thank you."

Dr. Cromwell shook Daniel's hand. "No problem. I'll see you all tomorrow, hopefully with more information. Sharon, you can go back and see your husband in a few minutes. A nurse will come and get you." Then he pivoted and left.

Sharon slumped into her chair, throwing her head forward into her palmed hands, and cried until a nurse came to fetch her. After wiping her tears away, she put on a brave face before allowing the nurse to take her through the swinging doors to Eric.

Rachel, Daniel, and Ashley all sat back down in their seats in unison. Only Sharon was allowed to see Eric. They would have to wait until morning. In a haze, the minutes passed. Rachel felt numb and confused. How quickly life changed. One minute you're young and in love and then, boom, the dam breaks.

Daniel finally spoke up. "Rachel, how long do you think you can stay in town?" Nervously shifting in his seat, he gnawed at his fingernail. "I think this whole thing with dad is going to be a long road. Mom will need all the extra help she can get."

Letting out a long breath, Rachel leaned forward. "I'm not sure." She glanced away from them. She had notified her work, managing to find people to pick up her shifts for the next week. Beyond that she wasn't sure how long they would hold her job. And Rachel loved her job. The thought of leaving it only made her spiral.

Rachel might not have a choice. Most likely, she would need to stay in Cloverton . . . indefinitely.

NYC was her home. Her life was there. But all of that might be gone. She tried not to think too far forward, but instead to simply take everything a day at a time. It was the only way she could deal with the entire situation.

"I found people to take my shifts for the week, but beyond this week, I really don't have the resources to give up many more shifts." Rachel wished she didn't have to worry about her finances at a time like this, but she did. "I only have a few days of leave. After I use those up, I don't get paid if I don't work."

Ashley wrapped her arm around Daniel's tense shoulders. "Together we can come up with some sort of game plan." Her glance danced between Daniel and Rachel. "When we know more about your dad's prognosis, we'll find a way to sort it all out."

"I only have so many sick days I can take." Daniel tightened his hands into fists, tapping them on top of his thighs. His jaw locked. "What are we going to do? All of us have other obligations, and you know Mom and Dad don't have the money to hire help."

"I know," replied Rachel, crossing her arms. Glancing out the window again, the sun began its ascent, filling the room with dawn light. It warmed her skin, and she took a moment to let it soak into her soul. Perhaps things weren't as dismal as they seemed. "All we can do at this point is hope things aren't as bad as they appear to be."

Daniel unlocked himself from Ashley's embrace, pacing back and forth. His nervous energy brought knots to Rachel's stomach. With nothing else to do and the future uncertain on so many levels, she curled up into a ball on the double wide chair and drifted off to sleep.

CHAPTER TWENTY

James entered his office the next morning in an extra grumpy mood. Besides the few texts with Rachel before he went to sleep, he hadn't heard from her. The last place he wanted to be was at work. His heart was in Cloverton with Rachel. Multiple times she had requested he come to be with her, but here he remained, working, like he always did.

Around noon, Robert popped his head into the doorway. "Do you have time to eat? I was going to go buy something off a food cart for lunch. We could discuss those additional changes that came in this morning while we wait."

"Sure." James stretched, twisting and turning his neck to get the kink out. Then he stood, grabbing his cell phone. "Is this about the change to the payment schedule?" He strode toward the door, both walking to the elevator.

"Yes." Robert hit the elevator button, shoving his hands back into his pockets. He watched the elevator lights changing numbers, getting closer to their floor. "Thoughts?"

Inwardly, James groaned. He rubbed the back of his neck with his hand. "I think if they're adamant about such a fast payment schedule, we could bring it up to our client. Though I don't understand their hurry."

"I think they're having money problems." The elevator dinged, and they entered. Robert continued speaking once they were alone in the moving elevator. "I get the impression they don't want to sell to our client, but the deal is out of financial necessity."

"I see," replied James. "No wonder they're being so pushy with their deadlines. The bank might be hassling them."

The two discussed the agreement for the rest of the elevator ride, continuing all the way outside. Spotting a food truck that sold chicken and waffles, James suggested it, and Robert agreed. Once they placed their order, James allowed himself to double check his phone to see if Rachel had texted him back. Nothing. Leaning against the food truck, his mind a thousand miles away, James half-listened as Robert rattled on about their current deal. On another day, discussing the intricacies of the deal would have invigorated James with its unique challenges. Not now. Not today.

Robert interrupted his scattered thoughts. "Everything okay?" He raised an eyebrow. "You seem to be elsewhere."

Their order was called, interrupting their conversation. Both walked to the window and grabbed their food, then made their way back to the courtyard by their building to find a bench to eat.

Once settled on a bench, James finally said, "My girlfriend Rachel . . ." He exhaled, wondering if he should continue.

Robert, while chewing, waved to him to go on.

"Her dad had a stroke. The prognosis isn't good. She asked me to be with her, but I told her I couldn't because of work and this case. I don't know." James gripped his still closed to-go box tightly. "I might lose her over this, and she's all I have."

Nodding, Robert finished chewing before he replied, "If she

asked you to be there, then you better be there." Nonchalantly, he shrugged and took another bite of his food.

"It isn't that easy. You know how this job can be." James placed his to-go box on the bench, placing his hands on both sides of himself. "I can't drop everything to be with her. That isn't how mergers work. The clients expect us to be available to them when they want us."

Robert scoffed. "I think there's more to this story than you're telling me." He cut into more of his waffles. "You could've asked me to work remotely for the week. You've proven your worth. I would've trusted you to get your work done from there."

"There's more," James paused. His chest pinched. The other piece, returning to Cloverton, danced through his psyche. "Her dad is at the same hospital where my mom passed away. Um—" James stammered. "I haven't been there since she passed. I don't know." He shook his head. "I know it isn't a big deal, but it just brings up a lot of things I've tried my best to forget."

Robert stopped mid-bite, lowering his fork back to his to-go box. "I see. I knew there was something more. I'm sorry for what you've gone through. Losing a parent is never easy." He wiped his face with his napkin. "Have you explained all of this to Rachel?"

"No," James quickly replied, glancing away, "I haven't." He kicked away a piece of trash in front of him with his shoe.

"You need to talk to her about all this." Robert scooted some of his food around with his fork. "I'd start with explaining everything you just told me, so Rachel understands better why you were hesitant to join her."

"Very true." James shifted in his seat. "I need to go be with Rachel. If you'll let me work remotely, I'll leave as soon as I can."

"Yes. Of course," Robert nodded, "I wish you luck with everything."

Rachel scrubbed the dishes in her parents' sink, lost in thought, missing James and wishing he was there.

"Here, I'll dry." With a towel in hand, Haley reached out to take the dish from her. "I think you've scrubbed that pot enough." She raised an eyebrow, eyeing her suspiciously.

Yesterday, Rachel had called Haley in desperation, bawling her eyes out about her dad's condition. He was still in the hospital and things weren't good. Paralyzed on half of his body, he might never walk or talk again. The doctors didn't sugarcoat the situation. Things might improve some, but her dad's life, and their lives, would all be different from here on out.

Haley, being the best friend in the world, packed up her baby and drove first thing in the morning to be with Rachel. Luckily, Haley's parents still lived in town, too, and were watching her little one for the day.

Flipping the water back on, Rachel rinsed the pot, then handed it to her. "I miss James." She exhaled, her body a tense ball of nerves. "I wish he was here."

Haley dried the pot. "I know." Haley, who knew Sharon's kitchen as well as Rachel did, opened the appropriate cupboard to put away the pot. "James should be here. I have no excuses for him, but I'm sure you'll figure things out when you get back to New York."

Rachel shook her head, turning off the water after squeezing soap onto her sponge. She moved on to the Pyrex pan, scrubbing it aggressively. "I might not go back to New York." She glanced over at Haley.

Haley leaned up against the counter, folding her arms. She waited for Rachel to continue.

"Mom needs me." Rachel's voice cracked. "As much as I don't want to, it might be time for me to come home."

"You sure about that?" Haley folded and refolded the towel in her hands. "I don't think your parents will want you to just up and leave your life there. Your job is there—and James. Are you willing to just walk away from all of that?"

"I feel like I don't have a choice." Rachel's shoulders drooped as the hefty weight of her life came crashing down on her. Tears stung the corners of her eyes. "My parents can't afford to hire help, and I'm a nurse after all." She swiped at her eyes. "Who's going to help them? Who?"

Rinsing the Pyrex pan, Rachel handed it to Haley with a shaky hand. Haley took it but set it on the counter without drying it. Instead, she pulled her closer for a hug. Rachel sobbed on her shoulder, allowing the jumble of emotions bottled up in her to come pouring out.

"Let it out." Haley rubbed her back in round, rhythmic circles. "You'll figure out what to do next."

The doorbell rang, interrupting their embrace. Rachel wiped away the last of her tears, straightening her shoulders. "I'll get that," Rachel said.

"I'll finish up in here," Haley replied as she picked up her towel and began to dry the Pyrex pan.

Rachel left the safety of the kitchen, wandering to the front door. Most likely, it was another delivery from the medical equipment store. Her parents' front living room had turned into a makeshift bedroom overnight to accommodate her dad's new hospital bed. The doorbell sounded again.

"Hold your horses. I'm coming." Rachel swung open the door, and there on the stoop was James. She wondered if she was dreaming. Her hand remained on the propped door, staring back at the entire image of him, in the flesh.

"You came," she breathed.

Her heartbeat rang in her ears as the tension dissipated from her shoulders.

"I came." James stared back at her, making her tingly all over.

Instantly, she forgave him. He might be a little late, but he was here, nonetheless.

James shuffled his feet and continued, "I'm sorry. I should've come the minute you asked me."

Interrupting their exchange, Haley called out from somewhere in the house. "Who is it?"

The floorboards creaked under her weight as Haley strode out toward the door. Rachel peered over shoulder, catching Haley's glance. Her jaw dropped when she saw James. The friends exchanged a look.

"I'll—" Haley backpedaled. "I'll get some dinner ready for everyone." She then pivoted and hurried back into the kitchen.

Rachel brought her attention back to James.

He ran a hand down the length of his face. "Haley came?" James blurted out.

"I asked her to come." With a shaky hand, Rachel smoothed the top of her hair. "I was a bit of a mess, and I needed a friend."

Shaking his head, James glanced out toward the sidewalk. He fiddled with the hem of his jacket. His shoulders drooped. "I hope I'm not too late." His voice cracked. "I wish I could properly explain how sorry I am. I should've come the first time you asked. I apologize. But this town . . ." He exhaled, bringing his glance back to her. "It's so hard for me to be here. I mean, my mom died in that hospital. I—I thought I couldn't—"

Whoosh. The words sucked the air out of her lungs. Stunned, Rachel paused. "I'm so sorry. I didn't know." She let go of the door, stepping onto the porch toward him, closing the gap between them. "You're here now."

Rachel reached out, tugging him closer to her. Their fingers interlocked. His familiar cologne tickled her nose, and she allowed herself to take in its scent.

"I wish it hadn't taken me so long to realize that you're the most important thing in my life." James reached out, tucking her hair behind her ear, cupping her cheek. "You're everything that matters." His words sent goosebumps down her back, traveling all the way to her toes. His eyes traveled the length of her face, scanning it.

"I'm glad you're here. It means the world to me." Rachel moistened her lips. "I've missed you."

"I've missed you too." James wrapped his arms around her waist, bringing her body tight against his.

Instantly, Rachel melted against him. With his arms supporting her, she was steadier than she had been all week. Everything would be okay because he was there beside her. Placing a hand against his chest, she tilted her head up, meeting his eyes.

James gulped, tracing the outline of her chin with his finger. "I'm going to kiss you now," he stated.

With a smile, Rachel replied, "You'd better."

Slowly, James leaned in, brushing his tongue along her bottom lip. The feeling of being home enveloped her and soon her lips parted, inviting him in. Her heart hammered. Knees buckled. She gripped a fist full of his shirt, tugging their bodies closer. Stumbling a few feet backward, Rachel leaned against the wall of the house for support. As Rachel kissed James, the worries of the past week became duller and more manageable. Time had no meaning. Everything would be okay if she had him in her life.

Then the world became clearer. Rachel had to move back home for the foreseeable future, possibly forever. Rachel broke their embrace, pulling away from the comfort of his body.

"I have to tell you—" Rachel tried to regain her breath as her mind raced with the injustice of it all.

James brushed a few strands of hair out of her eyes, tucking them behind her ear. "Tell me what?" His eyes searched her face for meaning.

Why did he have to look at her like that? It made her heart break into a million pieces. All her life she had searched for someone like him, and now life's challenges would pull them apart, making it impossible for them to be together. A sliver of hope beat within her heart. Maybe James could give up New York? Impossible. Even the thought seemed ridiculous to her. James had already told her he was never living in Cloverton. Her reality crashed down on her.

He touched his forehead to hers, taking her face into her hands. "Rachel," James whispered, "what is it?"

The magic was gone. Reality came back. Duty called. "I'm not going back to New York," Rachel stated. "Honestly, I don't know if I can ever go back."

The air became static, popping and sizzling with her revelation. His jaw dropped. Once she could no longer stare at the stunned look on his face, Rachel rested her head against his chest and sobbed.

CHAPTER TWENTY-ONE

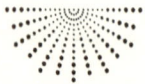

In a daze, James rhythmically ran his hands over Rachel's back as she cried. Rachel wasn't coming back to New York. The words whizzed around his mind as a thousand questions came in rapid succession. Surely, things weren't this dire. Or were they? His whole life was in New York, but it wouldn't mean anything if Rachel wasn't there with him. Visiting Cloverton was hard enough, but living here—impossible.

A shuffling sound in the front yard interrupted their embrace, and both turned, looking down at the walkway. A man stared back at them. James had a hazy memory of him from childhood.

Daniel paused at the bottom of the few stairs leading up to the porch. Fiddling with his keys, he finally shoved them into his pocket. Clearing his throat, he asked, "Who do we have here?"

"This is James." Rachel adjusted her shirt and smoothed out her hair. She jutted her chin. "He just arrived."

The siblings stared at each other as if a separate conversation was occurring via telepathy. James wanted to make a good impression on Rachel's family, even when he had a million questions running through his mind, so he reminded himself to be gracious.

"Yes." He held his hand out to Daniel. "I'm James. It's nice to meet you." He managed to smile.

Introductions were made and a few pleasantries were exchanged, but James could feel Daniel questioning his presence. Obviously, Rachel had informed them of James not coming when she originally wanted him there, and Daniel, being a protective brother, no doubt questioned James's intentions now.

"Ashley and Mom will be here in a few minutes. Mom's going to eat, then head back to the hospital." Daniel met James's glance, raising an eyebrow. "Are you staying for dinner?"

James looked to Rachel for approval. "If it's okay with Rachel," he said while maintaining eye contact with her.

Rachel nodded, giving his hand a squeeze. "Of course, come on in. Haley said she would get something started for everyone. Let's go see if she needs any help."

Daniel entered the house. Rachel and James filed in behind him. James tried to push his racing thoughts aside while he shut the door. Clearly, Rachel wasn't going to discuss her moving back to Cloverton until later. Hopefully they could find a minute to be alone to talk about it. But he'd have to wait. His stomach started eating itself, and he forced himself to temper his anxiety.

Joining Haley in the kitchen, she quickly put them to work to help set the table for dinner. Rachel and James worked in tandem silence. The bomb dropped from earlier created a palpable divide between them. So much had been left unsaid, but he had no choice but to be patient. James was placing water glasses on the table when he saw two women appear in the doorway to the dining room.

The older of the two women crossed her arms, eyeing them. "Rachel, I'm assuming this is James." Her voice lingered on his name, making it dangle in the air.

A small smirked settled on the face of the younger woman.

Rachel folded the cloth napkin in her hand, tucking it under the plate. "Yep. This is James." She continued to fold the next napkin, ignoring the gawking women.

"James," said Rachel's mom. "It's about time you showed up." Her words came out half joking, half serious.

"Mom," Rachel hissed, tilting her head to the side. Closing her eyes, she pinched the bridge of her nose.

After Rachel opened her eyes again, she introduced James to her mom, Sharon, and sister-in-law, Ashley. Interrupting their awkward exchange, Haley came in from the kitchen carrying a large platter with meat and potatoes on it.

"Dinner is ready," Haley announced as she placed the platter in the center of the table.

Sharon hugged Haley and thanked her.

Daniel entered, wrapping an arm around his wife's shoulders. Completely ignoring James, he asked Sharon and Ashley, "How did Dad seem today?"

Glancing up at Daniel, Ashley shrugged. "He's about the same."

Sharon sighed. Her shoulders drooping as she slumped into a seat. Resting her elbows on the table, she cradled her chin. "The future is bleak. I'm trying to not think too far ahead, or I might lose it. I mean, he can't even feed himself at this point."

All joined her, sitting down. James took the seat next to Rachel. Worry lines spread across Rachel's face, and James wanted nothing more than to ease some of the burden, but he had no idea what to do. He had very limited experience with family, especially in a situation like this one.

"I know. It's devastating," added Rachel. She reached across the table and gave Sharon's hand a squeeze. "But we're here to help you through it."

"I can't take care of him full-time on my own, and we can't afford a caretaker." Sharon, leaning forward, covered her face with her hands. Her voice cracked. "It's all too much." Then she started to cry.

It broke James's heart. The room became eerily quiet. Daniel cast his glance at his plate, while Ashley gnawed on her bottom lip. Haley fiddled with her silverware. Under the table, Rachel clasped and unclasped her hands.

Finally, Rachel broke the silence. Her face devoid of emotion, she announced, "I'm moving home." She kept her gaze glued to the platter of food.

Sharon peered up from her palmed hands. "No. No." She shook her head. "I can't let you do that. Your job and life are in New York. You love it there. I can't ask you to give all that up."

"You didn't ask," Rachel stated. Her voice was even and steady, though James saw her back stiffen. "I offered."

All turned their glance to James. His stomach plummeted and his skin itched. Uncomfortably, he shifted in his seat while tugging at his shirt collar. The question of what would happen to the two of them practically hung in the air. Quite frankly, he wondered too. His world was crumbling, and there was nothing he could do to stop it. Under the table his shaky hands formed tight fists, and James forced himself to breathe and appear calm.

"Now, let's eat before the food gets cold." Rachel motioned toward the food. "Haley was nice enough to make it for all of us."

Nobody moved or said anything. "Eat," Rachel said. The word hard and firm.

Slowly, Haley reached for the platter of meat and potatoes. She held it in front of Sharon for her to serve herself. While Sharon scooped some onto her plate, Haley glanced across the table at James. Their eyes met. And he knew. This was the end. He wanted to pound on the table and scream about the injustice of it all, but instead he ate his food, tasting nothing. The meal passed with awkward stops and starts of conversation. What does someone say when there is an elephant in the room? It didn't help that Rachel refused to even glance in his direction once.

After dinner finally ended, Haley said goodbye and left to

return to her parents' house. Next, Sharon exited with Daniel and Ashley for the hospital, leaving Rachel and James alone for the first time in hours. All whispered in hushed tones with Rachel before they left, while he waited for her on the living room couch. James was unraveling. His brow lathered itself with sweat. Hands clammy, James rubbed the back of his neck.

With the house finally quiet, he heard the grandfather clock in the foyer ticking in the background. James tried to concentrate on the rhythmic beat. Rachel came in, settling onto the couch next to him. She curled her legs under herself while she sipped on a mug of chamomile tea.

Resting his arm behind the back of the couch, James tried to find the words trapped deep inside of him. "I can't follow you here. My job—it just won't work. I can wait for you to return to New York, if you think you might come back . . "

"I don't think I'll ever go back. My mom needs me here." Rachel stared straight ahead at the smoldering logs in the fireplace. Her voice cracked. "I wish everything was different." She took a slow sip of her tea. Her eyes were misty. "I hope you understand how much I wish things weren't this way, but I don't have a choice."

"I wish they were different, too." James reached out, cupping her cheek. Rachel leaned into his hand, closing her eyes for a moment. "I love you so much. You're the only one I've ever really loved."

His words pierced the very air they breathed, whirling and twirling between them.

"But sometimes . . ." Rachel exhaled, shifting her body away from him so they were no longer touching. She placed her mug on the coffee table. "Sometimes love isn't enough."

If only things weren't this way, if only he wasn't held back from the darkness of his past. This place, this town, encapsulated years of heartache and pain. Every corner riddled him with anxiety, because here he was instantly the little boy who nobody loved. Coming was one thing, but living here permanently, never. He didn't have it in him.

"I can't quit my job." James tried to explain. "There aren't even any big law firms here."

Blinking rapidly, Rachel glanced up, fighting back tears. Then she cleared her throat. "I know. You can't move here, and I can't stay there." She shifted, meeting his gaze, placing a hand on his knee. "I wish I wasn't needed here, because I love you too."

The words gutted him, spiraling him to a tipping point. He was unsure if the dam within him would break or hold. Words would have revealed the pain, so instead of speaking, he wrapped his arm around her, pulling her tight against his chest. She clung to him while they both cried in a devastating goodbye.

CHAPTER TWENTY-TWO

The months that followed were a long string of blurry days. Rachel's dad was released from the hospital, taking up full-time residence in her parents' living room. Between Sharon and Rachel, his care consumed their entire lives. He needed help with even the simplest of tasks. Drained and emotional, Rachel tried her best to put on a brave face. Her entire life was gone, and her future was bleak. Every part of her missed the busy streets of New York, the smelly subway, crowded sidewalks, and . . . breakfast burritos. Not to mention, she longed for the busy days as a nurse in labor and delivery.

But, most of all, she ached for James.

Every minute of every day, she thought of him. She wondered if he had moved on and found someone new. Her mind ran rampant with the possible scenarios of his current life. A life where she wasn't a part of it. Their love story, as brilliant as it was in the beginning, crashed and burned at the first obstacle. Clearly, they weren't meant for the long haul. It didn't make it any easier, even when Rachel came to accept that not everyone gets their happily-ever-after. Sometimes life dealt you an unfair hand.

As bad as Rachel's life seemed, her mom's entire world had been rocked to its core. Rachel only hoped she could help her put the pieces back together. With no choice, they divided the work. Days were filled with various therapy appointments, feeding, and exercise schedules. Time passed, slowly but surely. Late at night, when Rachel had time to ponder everything, she forced herself to stop. Her life was passing her by. But there was nothing that could be done.

One night while cleaning up the kitchen alone, Rachel methodically wiped down the countertop. Sharon's voice startled her. Rachel peered over, finding her leaning against the doorway with arms crossed.

"I've been thinking . . ." Sharon's voice trailed off.

Rachel folded the rag in her hands, leaning her back against the kitchen sink. "And?" She raised an eyebrow.

"As much as I've appreciated your help with Dad, I think it's time for you to return to your life in New York." Sharon walked all the way into the kitchen, leaning against the countertop opposite her. "I can handle things here. It took me a while to find my footing, but I can take it from here."

Rachel exhaled. Her mind whirling in a million different directions. "Mom, you can't do all of this on your own. It's too much. Dad needs around-the-clock care. And it's taken the both of us working together to get it all done."

She wished this wasn't the case. Wished she could return to New York, her job, apartment, maybe even James. But her reality didn't include those things. It simply couldn't be.

"I know, but I can't sit by and watch you give up everything." Sharon gripped the counter on both sides of her. "You're miserable here. You walk around like a zombie with a face full of sadness. It's breaking my heart. You're my child, and I want you to be happy." She shook her head. Her voice cracked. "No, you need to go back to New York. Your job, life—everything is there. Maybe you could even reconcile things with James."

"Mom . . ." Rachel tilted her head to the side, pinching the bridge of her nose. Her heart wanted nothing more than to go back and figure out things with James. But he had walked away and never even attempted to contact her, not even to see if she was okay. He had moved on, so she needed to do the same.

Yes, she had told him to stay away, but Rachel hadn't truly expected that he would listen. If anything, she had hoped he'd fight for them to stay together, but both had mutually just given up. The distance with no foreseeable change made everything fizzle. Loudly, she exhaled. "That ship has sailed."

Sharon gnawed on her fingernail. "You need to at least try to get him back. You're so unhappy. I know it's because you want to be with him. I can't stand in the way of my daughter's chance at love."

Rachel glanced out the window, avoiding eye contact. "It wasn't meant to be. I'll find someone else." The words were like acid on her tongue. James was firmly embedded in her heart, but her mom didn't need to know how much she had given up by staying. "Dad needs me. You need me." The reality, at times, felt like a thousand bricks stacked up on her shoulders.

"I talked to our insurance company and to the social security office." Sharon glanced down, wringing her hands together. "They've been helping me to apply for some assistance. They think I can qualify for a caretaker a few hours a day."

Rachel's jaw dropped. "When did you do all of this?"

"Daniel and Ashley have been assisting me with all the paperwork. We all want you to not to be stuck with this burden." Sharon gripped her forearm. "You were always bigger than this town. You come alive when you are in New York City. I can't take that away from you."

"I don't know if I can go back." Rachel shook her head, casting her gaze away. "Amber might have found someone to sublease my room. The hospital probably already filled my position . . . I . . ."

A thousand other what-ifs ran unrestrained through her mind. James probably had moved on; he might even be with someone new.

"The hospital is hiring. I checked their website. Three positions are available in labor and delivery." Sharon raised an eyebrow. "Now call Amber and see if you can get your room back, then once you are back in New York and back in the swing of things, call James."

Rachel forced a laugh, which fell flat. "You make it all sound so easy."

"It could be. Go." Sharon embraced Rachel. "Go live your life. I'll be okay. Promise."

"I love you, Mom." Rachel hugged Sharon back.

"I love you too."

In the crowded restaurant, Ryan asked over the noise. "How long has it been since you've seen Rachel?"

James let out a long breath, the familiar pinch of his chest, making him all aware of the agony of the last several months. "Five months."

He took a drink, reverting his attention back to the basketball game playing on the big screen on the wall facing them.

"Five months," Ryan repeated. He took the last bite of his pizza, then wiped his face with a napkin. "Have you gone out with anyone since then?"

"No." The word came out harsher and more defensive than James wanted. "I'm not ready."

James didn't add that he never would be. Nor did he divulge what an idiot he had been in letting Rachel go in the first place. He shook his head at his actions. If he had any sort of foresight, he would have tried to make things work, offered to try things long distance. Some of Rachel would've been better than none.

"Chloe has a friend she wants you to meet," Ryan stated as he grabbed another slice of combo pizza off the metal pan sitting on the table between them. "Apparently, she's an attorney too." He casually took a bite of his pizza while watching the game.

Grabbing a slice of pizza too, James set it on his plate. "I appreciate Chloe thinking of me, but I don't know." He inwardly groaned at the idea of dating again. "I'm not really looking to date."

Over the past several months of Ryan and Chloe dating, James had come to see how perfect they were for each other. Chloe was a wonderful person, and he knew she wouldn't set him up with just anyone. Maybe he'd have to force himself to try again.

"Come on. We'll all go to the Yankees game together. It's chill, low key. No pressure." Ryan shrugged. "It could be fun." Then he shoved him. "And it could get you out of this rut you are in right now."

"I'm not in a rut." Wiping his face with his napkin, James continued, "I'm just not interested in dating."

Ryan scoffed. "You're in a rut." He slapped him on his back. "But that's why you have me. I'm going to help you get out of it. That's what friends are for."

Their team scored a three-pointer, and both cheered and exchanged high fives.

Diverting the conversation away from himself, James asked, "Enough about me and my lack of a social life. How about you and Chloe? You're practically attached at the hip. Do you think Chloe is the one?"

Shifting in his seat, Ryan glanced at him, then back at the game. "I do." Ryan ran a hand through his hair. "I think I'm going to marry her."

James's jaw dropped. "Wow," James finally managed. He made himself smile. "That's wonderful news." Slowly, he took another bite of his pizza. "I'm happy for you two."

"Thanks." Ryan took a drink of his soda. "And to think it all started at our ten-year reunion." He shook his head, eyes glued to the big screen.

James cheered at a successful free throw. "What are the odds?"

The thought whizzed through him, making his stomach clench tight. The familiar pinch in his shoulder blades came back. *Rachel. Rachel. Rachel.*

"Higher than you would think," replied Ryan.

Before James could ask what he meant, the basketball game went into overtime. The subject of women was dropped, and James figured Ryan had let it go. But as they filed out of the restaurant, Ryan adjusted his jacket. "I'm setting up this double date to the Yankees game, whether you like it or not. Next week."

James didn't argue, bidding Ryan goodbye.

CHAPTER TWENTY-THREE

Trudging up her apartment stairs, her arms screamed from the weight of her luggage. Out of breath, Rachel tapped on the door with her foot.

Within seconds, the door opened. "Rachel!" Amber grinned. Then she reached out to help her with her bags. "You're back."

Wiping her sweaty brow, Rachel replied, "I am. It's good to be home." She slid past the door Amber held open, dropping her bags by it.

"I'm glad. Come." She waved her over. "Let's sit." Rachel joined her on the couch. Amber continued, "The person I subleased your room to turned out to be a total nightmare. She left her dirty clothes all over the bathroom floor, played her music at full volume late into the night. No, thank you. I was more than happy to give her notice to hit the road."

Rachel laughed. "I'm happy it didn't work out."

"So," Amber slapped her on the knee, "what's the latest with you and James? I bet he's glad you're back in town. I'm sure he's missed you being away for so long."

"We . . ." Rachel wrung her hands together, avoiding eye

contact. "We broke up. I haven't seen him since he came to see me at my parent's house, way back in the beginning."

Being back here, being this close to James, was doing funny things to her. In Cloverton, she pushed the memory of him away whenever he popped into her mind. Not here. Not in this city, *their* city. The very air in her lungs seemed heavy with memories of him. Here, it was impossible to forget about him. Her mind became a jumbled mess. She wondered if he was dating someone new, and if, on the odd chance she ran into him, highly unlikely to happen here, what she would say to him.

Regardless, Rachel was happy to be back in New York City. Just getting off the plane at JFK had brought a smile to her face, and she hadn't had anything to smile about in a long time. Even if she never saw James again, at least she knew this city was where she belonged. Though she loved Cloverton, being there all those months had made her feel restless and incomplete.

"I'm sorry." Amber blinked. With a face full of compassion, Amber added, "I didn't know. I didn't mean to bring up a sensitive subject."

Rachel rubbed her hands back and forth over her thighs, anxiety pulsating through her. She rapidly stood. "There's nothing for you to be sorry for. Things between us didn't work out." She shrugged, trying desperately to appear calm and collected, and not like her entire world might crumble again. "I'm going to go unpack. I have my first shift tonight."

"Tonight." Amber made a tsk sound with her tongue. "That soon?"

"Yep." Rachel grabbed her pile of bags. "I depleted my savings during my stay at my parents', and that included my vacation fund for Barcelona. I'm trying not to think about the fact I might never actually get to go there."

"Understood." Amber grabbed her laptop off the coffee table, opening it.

Rachel dragged her bags out of the living room toward her room.

Interrupting her, Amber said, "And Rachel . . ."

Rachel pivoted, looking over her shoulder at Amber. "Yeah?"

"Don't worry. You'll get to Barcelona someday." Amber smiled. "You aren't a person to give up on a dream just when things get hard. It's one of the things I admire the most about you."

"Thanks," Rachel replied.

She was grateful for how much things had shifted between her and her roommate. And James had been an integral part of the reason.

Later in the afternoon, after she unpacked and everything was back in its place, Rachel changed into her scrubs. Practically giddy, she pulled her hair up into a messy bun. Staring at her reflection in the mirror, she attempted to smooth out the loose strands while ignoring her haggard appearance. The last several months had been a long stream of hard and exhausting days, and the toll was written all over her face. She smiled at her image, making the reflection of herself brighten. Soon, she'd be back in the swing of things with work and her normal routine. Maybe even the light in her eyes would return, replacing her hollowed-out image.

Her phone rang. She picked it up off the vanity, scanning the screen. She hit accept and put the phone on speaker. "Haley."

Rachel applied a little lip gloss. She smacked her lips together, then flicked off the bathroom light, entering her bedroom.

"Have you called him yet?" asked Haley.

Rachel laughed and placed her phone on her bed. "Well, hello to you, too."

She retrieved her most comfortable pair of sneakers. Sitting on the edge of her bed, Rachel put them on one at a time.

"Yeah, yeah. Hello," Haley mockingly replied. "Answer me, does James know you're back in New York?"

Rachel took the phone off speaker. Cradling it in the crook of her neck, Rachel tied her shoes. "I literally arrived three hours ago. So, no. I haven't called James, nor do I plan on it anytime soon. We broke up, and he's made no attempt to contact me. Not even to get an update on my dad. There's nothing there. It's best to leave it alone."

"I think we can both agree he wasn't the smartest, letting you go so easily, but you have to at least text him and meet up with him once." Haley paused, then blew out a long breath. "You two are meant to be together."

"Okay Haley." Rachel rolled her eyes while she shifted the phone to the opposite shoulder. "I've got to run. I start my first shift tonight." She stood, gathering up her purse and keys.

"Text him," Haley forcefully added.

"No," Rachel said. "Bye Haley." She hung up.

Rachel wasn't calling or texting anyone. Her bank account was down to two hundred bucks. James, and romance with anyone for that matter, was at the bottom of her list.

James double-checked the seat number on his Yankee ticket, making sure it matched up with the proper queue. Once he confirmed he was in the correct tunnel, he passed through it until it gave way to the seats and baseball field below. Scanning the rows of seats, he spotted Ryan and Chloe already in their seats with the woman who apparently would be his date.

What was he doing? James didn't have any real interest in meeting anyone. Why had he even agreed to this whole thing? *Don't focus on that. Focus on being out with some friends. Anything to forget about Rachel.*

Inhaling, James took the stairs down to the proper row. He caught Ryan's eye. "Hello." He held his hand up in a wave.

Ryan grinned, standing. "James. You made it."

Chloe and her friend, Lacey, turned, eyeing him. Lacey had brown wavy hair and a nice smile.

Over the roaring crowd, James replied, "I did."

They all stood, allowing him to pass by. He settled into the seat at the end next to Lacey, who sat next to Chloe along with Ryan on the other end.

After the introductions were made, they focused on watching the game.

It was hard for James to talk to Lacey with how loud it was. The few times he tried, they were interrupted by plays happening on the field. In between innings, James took Lacey to get some food. Lacey seemed kind, but the conversation was stilted and difficult. The two had very little in common besides both being attorneys, which—no offense to her—he was looking for a little bit of variety in his rather drab life. Clearly, they weren't a match, which was fine by him.

After the game ended, they all walked toward the exit along with all the other fans. It was tight and crowded. "I almost forgot to tell you—" Chloe spoke over her shoulder as they weaved through the sea of people until they found an opening.

Once out of the stadium, they had a little bit more room.

James shoved his hands into his pockets. "What did you forget to tell me?"

Chloe glanced over at Ryan, who was a few feet in front of them, deep in conversation with Lacey. She gnawed on her bottom lip, leaning in a bit closer. Chloe whispered, "I ran into Rachel."

James stopped right in his tracks. Chloe halted next to him while Ryan and Lacey continued, melting further into the crowd. "When? Back in Cloverton?"

He remembered hearing something a few weeks back about Ryan and Chloe going home to visit their parents.

"No." Chloe adjusted her purse. "I wasn't sure if I should tell you or not." On her tiptoes, she peered above the sea of people, looking for Ryan and Lacey. "I saw her yesterday, getting off the subway."

"In New York?" His voice cracked as his eyes dilated.

He began to walk again, dragging his feet. Chloe trailed along beside him. Rachel was back. After all this time?

"Yes." Her eyes skimmed across him, studying his reaction. "In New York."

"Um—just—how long?" James ran a hand through his hair, then down the length of his face. His heart raced.

On her tiptoes, Chloe looked up, searching above the heads of those in front of them. "I don't know how long she's been here, but she's here—and for good, from what I gathered."

James remained speechless. Finally, he cleared his throat and asked, "Is her dad still alive?"

Chloe nodded. "Yes, but he never recovered from the stroke and still needs constant care. Rachel mentioned her family received some aid to pay for a part-time caretaker. I think it was enough for her to come back."

"I'm glad to hear he's still alive." James moved his gaze to the throngs of people in from of them. "I can't believe Rachel's back. She told me she wasn't ever returning, and I believed her."

"I think you should call her." Chloe spotted Ryan and Lacey and waved. "What do you have to lose?"

Ryan and Lacey spotted them too and waited several yards in front of them.

James waved too, but then turned his gaze back to Chloe. "But you just set me up with your friend."

"Yeah, and you two have nothing in common. I was just trying to get you out of the house and over Rachel." Chloe gave him a once over, before shaking her head. "But seeing Rachel, and now you—I can see I was wrong to think you two could ever be with anyone but each other."

They caught up with Ryan and Lacey, ending their conversation. His mind reeled. James couldn't remember anything they talked about on the rest of the way to the subway. All he could think about was Rachel somewhere in the city. His city. Their city. If she was back, he wasn't going to be the fool he had been before. This time, he would find her and tell her he had never stopped loving her. Even more importantly, he would apologize for not fighting for her. He'd even say he'd choose Cloverton if it meant they could be together.

CHAPTER TWENTY-FOUR

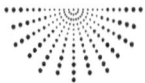

Being back at work full-time was exhausting, but she was happy to be delivering babies and visiting with her co-workers. If only James didn't live here too, because he seemed to be lurking on every corner. Running into Chloe a few days ago, in a city where that hardly ever happens, sent her into a James-loving tailspin. Chloe alluded to the fact he still was hung up on her. If that was true, why hadn't he contacted her at least once in the last six months?

You told him you were staying in Cloverton. Forever. You gave him no choice. His job and life are here.

Tired and hungry, Rachel rode the elevator to the hospital lobby. She shook her head, pushing out the constant thoughts of James, reminding herself their relationship was only a blip in her life.

The elevator doors swung open and Rachel spilled out. Halfway across the lobby, she spotted him.

James.

There in his hunky glory. Her heart tripled its speed, while her insides did a weird twist. Surely, it couldn't be this easy.

Could it? The air thickened. As she strode toward him, it was only him and her, and she hated that it was enough.

Rachel stopped in front of him, fiddling with the ends of her sweater. "James, what . . ." Her words came out more breathless than she would have liked. "What are you doing here?"

James held up a to-go bag. "I heard you were back in town." He shifted his weight and looked apprehensive. "I contacted Haley on social media. She helped me find out your schedule."

Rachel crossed her arms. "I don't even know what to do with that information."

"Don't worry about the details." James pulled out a breakfast burrito from the bag, holding it out to her. "Here, I know you're always hungry when you get off your shift, and I didn't forget that the breakfast place you like is open 24/7. Also, I didn't forget food was your love language."

In a daze, Rachel took the burrito from him. "I still don't understand. I haven't talked to you in months and then you show up out of the blue. And what?" She paused, shaking the burrito in her hand. "We pick up where we left off? How did you even know I was back?"

"Chloe told me she ran into you, and just knowing you were so close. . ." James ran a hand through his hair and shifted his weight. "I had to see you. I've missed you."

Rachel rolled her eyes as anger seeped into her veins. The last several months had been awful. James abandoned her when she needed him the most. Yeah, she had told him they couldn't be together. But she hadn't expected him to give up on them so easily. How could she possibly reconcile things with him? What would happen the next time they hit a rough patch? Would he leave her?

Rachel huffed, whipping her hair over her shoulder. "I—I—no. Just no." She walked toward the sliding glass doors, crossing through them to the outside. Squeezing the breakfast burrito tightly in her hand, she opened her purse and dropped it inside.

James jogged to catch up with her. "Wait." he called out.

Refusing to turn around, Rachel walked briskly toward her subway stop. James eventually fell into step next to her, but she refused to look over at him.

James said, "Please, can't we try again? I never stopped loving you. Nothing matters anymore. Because . . ." He stammered. "Because I don't have you in my life."

"I, uh . . ." Rachel stumbled over her words.

Heart hammering, Rachel stopped in the middle of the sidewalk. People dipped and dived around them. Her temples pulsated in her ears as she met his gaze. He saw her. The sounds of the city became silent. In a city full of people, for a blink, it was only him standing in front of her, asking her to try again. Tears stung the corners of her eyes. She gritted her teeth, hating how vulnerable she appeared.

For the past several months, Rachel had been sad and lonely without James, missing him and longing for him. Conveniently, now that the hard part was in the rear-view mirror, he came waltzing back. Nothing could ever be the same, because her life would never be the same. It was impossible. She had changed. Her dad would never recover. In the future, she might be called upon to return home again.

"James, I don't know." Rachel ran a hand through her hair, shaking off the whole idea of them together.

She strode toward the subway again. James matched her speed, step for step. Arriving at the subway tunnel, Rachel took the stairs at a fast pace. "Thanks for the burrito." She spoke over her shoulder. "But let's leave the past in the past."

Her heart clenched. She hated herself for speaking words she would regret later. But it couldn't be this easy for him, not when her heart had been broken into a thousand pieces.

"No," James stated. The throng of people moved in and out of them on the stairs. Coming and going. James spoke louder, over the heads of those passing by. "I'm sorry. I handled the whole situation wrong. I should've fought for you. I should've moved heaven and earth for us to be together. I didn't then, but I won't make that mistake again. I'll move to Cloverton. I'll do it. I regret not choosing you. Please."

The stairs ended, flattening out to a long hallway leading to the subway station. Rachel flashed her metro card in front of the portal. James fumbled around, digging into his pocket for his own card. He flashed it. She continued all the way to the correct subway platform before she stopped. Breathless, James joined her.

Shoving her metro card back into her purse, Rachel zipped it closed. She fiddled with her purse strap, hiking it back up her shoulder. "I don't think that's a good idea. We're"—she waved a finger between them—"we're not a good idea."

Pivoting, she refused to look at him. Instead, she kept her eyes glued to the tracks. James, this close to her, was breaking down her resolve. Even in the stinky subway station, Rachel smelled his intoxicating scent. Even months later, she longed for the feel of his stubble under her thumb. His lips on hers. The sound of his laugh, and the pleasure of his company. Dang, she wanted it all. She wanted him.

"And why not?" James reached out to touch her, but stopped himself, clenching his hand into a fist before shoving it into his pocket.

"Because." Her voice cracked. Rachel met his gaze, making a fire rage in her gut. "I don't know what I would do if I lost you again. I wouldn't survive." She gnawed on her bottom lip, holding back the powerful burst of emotions trying to wiggle their way out.

"I still love you, Rachel. Every day, I have woken up thinking about you, wondering if you were okay. You told me you were never coming back." He glanced out at the tracks, shaking his head. "You told me to give you a clean break, so I did. I can see now how wrong I was." James reverted his gaze back to her.

Their eyes locked. The air crackled and buzzed with electric energy. "I should've not given up on us. I should've found a way for us to be together . . . in Cloverton. I didn't do it then, but I'll do it now. If you'll only let me."

She sighed. "But you hate Cloverton." Rachel's voice lowered. "I couldn't do that to you."

"I know . . ." His voice trailed off. The sound of the subway approaching filled the space between them. He waited for it to stop in front of them. Then James spoke louder and stronger. "But I'll move there. I'll live there. If it means I get to be with you, then I'll do it. Then I'll choose Cloverton. Because I choose you."

People poured out of the subway. Rachel stumbled forward after getting shoved by tired commuters, forcing her to grip onto his forearm. "I don't want to live there, at least not right now," she yelled over the roar of the crowd. Swiftly, the subway doors closed. She watched as the train pulled away from the platform and disappeared into the darkness of the long, seemingly endless tunnel. Once gone, she peered back at him. "Being home for all these months, I've realized this is where I belong. Someday I might want to go back to Cloverton, but for now, NYC is home."

"What about your dad?" James wrapped an arm around her shoulder. "Who's taking care of him?"

She melted against his arm. "My brother and his wife helped my mom apply for some assistance for at-home care." Rachel gnawed on her bottom lip. A stream of remembrance of his touch, his kisses, flooded her mind. "It isn't enough to cover everything, but it was enough for me to come back here."

"I can help." James tucked some loose strands of her hair behind her ear. His fingers lingered by her ear, making her suck in the air. A fire raged in her gut.

She swallowed. "Help with what?" croaked Rachel.

"All of it. Carrying the burden, money, I have a ton of it and no family to spend it on. It's been only me all these years."

James tugged her waist closer, bringing her hip to hip. Rachel twisted to meet his body, resting her palm flat on his chest. Her fingertips picked up the steady pace of his pulse. His familiar spicy scent made her nostrils flare.

He continued, "Let me help you. I can pay for extra help."

"I can't let you pay for my dad's care." Rachel rubbed her hand back and forth over the ridges of his sweater, casting her eyes down. "We aren't even married. It wouldn't be right. I can't accept your money, even if my parents do need it."

Without hesitation, James stated, "Then, let's get married."

Startled, Rachel blinked. "What?" Her pulse thundered in her ears, making it hard to be sure she heard him correctly.

"Marry me," James repeated.

Nervously, Rachel laughed. "Marry you? You can't be serious."

James moved his hands from her waist to both of her shoulders. "I am." His gaze locked hers. "Marry me. Be with me. Choose me. We'll figure out the rest together, but let me help you. Let your family become my family. I don't have one, and I've been alone far too long. I love you, Rachel. I've loved you every day for as long as I can remember. And I promise to love you every day till the day I die, if you'll only let me."

Another subway train rolled to a stop beside them. A long stream of people poured out, parting around them. Rachel wrapped her arms tighter around his middle. "I love you too."

"Then marry me." James's hands glided from her shoulders down the length of her arms, stopping at her waist.

Rachel couldn't help but smile. "Fine." She threw up her hand. "Let's get married."

In one swift movement, James swept her up into his arms, twirling her around. "I'm getting married," he shouted. His voice echoing down the course of the subway tunnel.

Someone started to clap, then another joined in. Soon the space rang with the noisy sounds of clapping and cheering.

Rachel's head spun as he twirled her. Eventually, James stopped spinning her. Her feet hit the ground again.

"I love you," James whispered into her ear. "I choose you. I choose wherever you are, I'm there." Then he kissed her quickly on the lips.

Rachel stated, "I choose you too. I love you back."

Then she leaned in, her lips touching his, finally satisfying the need which pulsated through her. His lips parted hers as his tongue dove inside. Every sweep of his tongue increased the pace of her heart. His hands dove into her hair while his thumbs massaged her temples. Palming his sweater, Rachel brought him closer to taste all of him. The outside world became dimmer. Her axis tilted off course, moving back onto the one that spun around him and her.

In a city with millions of people, in that beautiful moment, it was only her and James kissing. Like it was the first time. Like today was a new beginning. Like everything in the past was in the past. Like their love was enough. And it was.

EPILOGUE

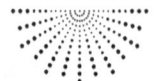

Tiles of blue, red, and orange cut into beautiful mosaics lined the park walls outside of the Gaudi Museum House. James fingered the edges of the tiles while admiring the magnificent design. Up close, one could see the various patterns printed on each broken piece of tile. Then when one stepped further back, the distinct artwork and brilliance of the architecture design came to life before your very eyes.

Along the path, James walked hand in hand with Rachel. A leisurely stroll, on a beautiful sunny day. From this viewpoint, in Park Güell, one could see the entire city of Barcelona.

Rachel stopped at the highest point, taking in the view. "This is as breathtaking as I imagined." She tilted her head toward him, smiling.

Sunlight cast its brilliant glow, making her and the entire colorful city sparkle. Taking a mental picture, James wanted to remember Rachel like this forever: young, carefree, and vibrant.

James squeezed her hand. "I have to admit," his glance swung from the view to Rachel, "I'm beginning to see why this city was on your top places to visit."

It was the final day of their honeymoon. Their time had been spent visiting all the places on Rachel's bucket list. Places she had been dreaming about and saving for, for years. La Sagrada Familia and La Costa Brava were their first stops. Next, they ate and shopped on their way down Las Ramblas. The Casa Batlló and Casa Milà were his favorite, while Rachel adored La Sagrada Familia.

If it had been up to James, he would have gone on their honeymoon to Tahiti and stayed in one of those little huts built right over the water. But being here, seeing the excitement on Rachel's face as a dream of hers came true, beat the crystal-clear waters of the beach any day of the week.

Wrapping an arm around James's waist, Rachel rested her head on his shoulder. "See?" She tilted her chin up, meeting his gaze. "I knew you'd love it here."

James kissed her on the temple, pulling her tighter against his side. "I do love it here." He sighed contentedly. "But mostly I love being here with you." Brushing some hairs out of her eyes, he tucked them behind her ear. Then he finally rested his hand behind her neck. "We could've honeymooned in Winnemucca for all I cared."

"*Winnemucca.*" Rachel gawked, playfully hitting him on the chest. "Where in the heavens is Winnemucca?"

"Nevada," James deadpanned. "Trust me, it's nothing to write home to Mom about."

Rachel laughed. "Well, I'm glad we didn't go there."

"Me too." James cupped the back of her neck. His fingers twisted into her hair. Rachel placed a hand on his chest. "But seriously, being here with you, married to you . . ." His voice caught in his throat. He cleared it. "It's a dream come true."

"Ahh," Rachel leaned in closer, giving him a quick peck. "I love you, James. Thanks for marrying me."

"Anytime," James whispered. "I choose you every day."

Then he crossed the divide which held them apart, allowing his lips to dance with hers. Rachel melted against his chest. Her fingers dove into his hair. He leaned against the tiled pony wall overlooking the city, deepening their kiss. His tongue swept her lower lip. Rachel felt warm and steady in his arms. Breathing in her luscious scent, he bathed in the feeling of love, acceptance, and belonging. In this moment, where it was only them, James held everything that mattered.

MEET THE AUTHOR

Emi Hilton is a California native who was born at March Airforce Base, while her father was an Officer in the US Army Combat Engineer Battalion. With an English Professor for a mother, Emi followed in her footsteps and graduated from Brigham Young University in English. While in college, she took a year and a half break from her studies to serve as a full-time missionary for her church in the Canary Islands. Emi writes sweet contemporary romance novels. Her debut novel, *Memories in Morro Bay*, was nominated for a Whitney Award. When Emi isn't writing, she enjoys training for marathons, fishing off local piers with her husband and three sons, or visiting her other love, Spain.

OTHER TITLES FROM 5 PRINCE PUBLISHING

www.5princebooks.com

Spring Showers *Sarah Dressler*
Secret Admirer Pact *Bernadette Marie*
The Publicity Stunt *Bernadette Marie*
A Trace of Romance *Ann Swann*
Descendants of Atlantis *Courtney Davis*
Holiday Rebound *Emily Bybee*
Rewriting Christmas *S.E. Reichert & Kerrie Flanagan*
Butterfly Kisses *Courtney Davis*
Leaving Cloverton *Emi Hilton*
Beach Rose Path *Barbara Matteson*
Aristotle's Wolves *Courtney Davis*
Christmas Cove *Sarah Dressler*
A Twist of Hate *T.E. Lorenzo*
Composing Laney *S.E. Reichert*
Firewall *Jessica Mehring*
Vampires of Atlantis *Courtney Davis*
A Rocky Mountain Romance *Jessica Mehring*
A Copper Penny Christmas *Ann Swann*